Jamie and I started padd...... canoe shot forward. With a gl............ toward my brothers, as I freed a hand to give them a last wave, I saw Burnt Paw in the river. Waterworthy as any muskrat, he was paddling after us with all his might.

I stopped paddling, I was laughing so hard. "Jamie!" I cried. "Look behind us!"

Here came that mongrel, with only his black-and-white face above water, his ears hinged forward with determination. The shore was slipping away; my brothers were bent over laughing. We were about to be swept into the boils at the edge of the main current.

Jamie spun the canoe sideways so that Burnt Paw would have a wider target. I stowed my paddle and made the catch. "Down the Yukon!" Jamie shouted. "Three for Nome!"

BOOKS BY WILL HOBBS

DOWN THE YUKON

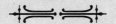

WILL HOBBS

■ HarperTrophy®
An Imprint of HarperCollinsPublishers

Down the Yukon
Copyright © 2001 by Will Hobbs
All rights reserved. No part of this book may be used or reproduced
in any manner whatsoever without written permission except in the case
of brief quotations embodied in critical articles and reviews.
Printed in the United States of America. For information address
HarperCollins Children's Books, a division of HarperCollins Publishers,
10 East 53rd Street, New York, NY 10022.

Library of Congress Cataloging-in-Publication Data
Hobbs, Will.
    Down the Yukon / Will Hobbs.
        p.   cm.
    Sequel to: Jason's gold.
    Summary: In the wake of Dawson City's Great Fire of 1899, sixteen-year-
old Jason and his girlfriend Jamie canoe the Yukon River across Alaska in
an epic race from Canada's Klondike to the new gold fields at Cape Nome.
    ISBN 0-688-17472-8 — ISBN 0-06-029540-6 (lib. bdg.)
    ISBN 0-380-73309-9 (pbk.)
    1. Nome Region (Alaska)—Gold discoveries—Juvenile fiction. [1. Nome
Region (Alaska)—Gold discoveries—Fiction.   2. Yukon River (Yukon and
Alaska)—Fiction.   3. Racing—Fiction.   4. Contests—Fiction.   5. Voyages
and travels—Fiction.]   I. Title.
PZ7.H6524 Dr   2001   00-044863
[Fic]—dc21   CIP
                                                                          AC

11 12 13 LP/BR 10 9 8
First Harper Trophy edition, 2002
❖
Visit us on the World Wide Web!
www.harperchildrens.com

to Richard Peck,
kind and generous friend

There's a land where the mountains are nameless,
*   And the rivers all run God knows where;*
There are lives that are erring and aimless,
*   And deaths that just hang by a hair;*
There are hardships that nobody reckons;
*   There are valleys unpeopled and still;*
There's a land—oh, it beckons and beckons,
*   And I want to go back—and I will.*

from "The Spell of the Yukon"
by Robert W. Service

JASON AND JAMIE'S NORTHLAND

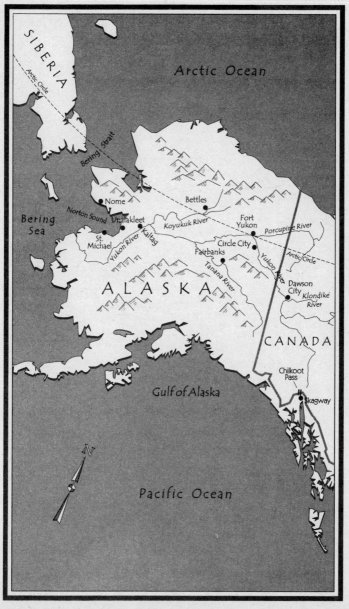

DOWN THE YUKON

ONE

The trouble started over a mongrel dog, small, mostly black, shorthaired and shivering. Without the fur to keep itself warm or the size to pull a sled, it had no business being in the North. How an animal so unsuited to living in the shadow of the Arctic Circle ever made it all the way to the Klondike is anyone's guess.

The gold rush had dumped a legion of abandoned dogs in Dawson City. They were a noisy, thieving bunch generally ignored by the population, including me. I no longer had the heart for dogs. During my struggle to catch up with my brothers in Dawson City, I'd lost a magnificent husky, as fine an animal as ever drew breath.

His name was King. The two of us had clawed our way over the Chilkoot Pass late in the fall of '97, only to lose our race with freeze-up on the Yukon. On New Year's Eve, that's when I lost King. More than a year later I missed him nearly as much as I missed Jamie Dunavant, the raven-haired Canadian girl I'd met along the trail.

Jamie was performing thousands of miles south, bringing the Klondike to the big cities. She was famous. Jamie had first become a sensation right in Dawson City, on the stage of the Palace Grand Theater. "The Princess of Dawson," that's what the miners called her.

Man, oh man, how I missed her.

Jamie's theater, as I thought of the Palace Grand, is where I found myself on a Saturday evening in March of '99. Strange to think that an hour later, a chance encounter with a dog would steer my brothers and me onto the road to disaster. Abraham, Ethan, and I were marveling at moving pictures, the first we'd ever seen. New inventions reached "the San Francisco of the North" surprisingly fast.

After the moving pictures, the owner of the Palace Grand entertained the audience with one of his shooting demonstrations. Arizona Charlie's target was a glass ball that his underdressed wife held between her thumb and forefinger. From clear across the stage, time after time, the old frontiersman never missed.

As the crowd spilled out into the subzero chill of Dawson's Front Street, the excited talk produced a cloud of vapor that fell as frost all around us. With buildings just on one side of Front Street and the other side being the riverbank, I could see the jagged ice ridges out on the frozen Yukon all lit by moonlight. Breakup, I was thinking, was only two months and a couple of weeks away.

While my brothers were trading guesses about the workings of the motion-picture projector, I was picturing those few freckles on Jamie's nose, her smile, her hair black as a raven's wing. For the thousand-and-first time I was pondering whether she really would return to the Golden City as she'd vowed.

Back in the fall, with Jamie gone only a few months, I was certain I'd see her walk down the gangplank of the first steamboat up from the Pacific. The endless winter darkness, however, had all but snuffed out my optimism. By March, despite the increasing daylight and the promise of breakup on the Yukon, I had little hope. Sometimes I doubted whether Jamie Dunavant even remembered me.

It wasn't often that Ethan or I had an excuse to visit dance-hall row. Abraham had laid down the law concerning drinking, gambling, and dollar dances. We were going to live by the code that our long-dead father had taught us, so help us God.

So far we had, though I could tell that Ethan, who had a fun-loving streak as long as Abraham's was short, was chafing at the harness. He resented Abe always playing the patriarch. At twenty-five, Abraham was oldest by only two years, while Ethan was nothing if not a full-grown man, burly and bearded and well over two hundred pounds. At sixteen I'd come into my full strength, but I hadn't yet succeeded in wrestling him to the ground.

As we passed by the entrance of the Monte Carlo, the fateful mongrel was padding down the boardwalk in our direction. I noticed the dog pausing here and there to look up at passersby with half-hopeful, half-wary eyes. Its face was split down the middle, half white and half black. Otherwise it was black except for white paws. The mutt's skinny excuse for a tail was bent at the halfway mark, broken maybe by a slamming door.

Its gaze met Ethan's. The white side of the dog's face

had an eye that was uncannily blue; the eye on the black side was brown.

Ethan slowed to a shuffle. "That animal's all ribs. Look how he's shivering, Jason."

"Nobody's going to skin him for a fur coat," I remarked.

A knot of men who'd just emerged from one of the saloons was joking about the weather warming up, which it had, from fifty degrees below zero to around twenty below. One of them, a tall, lanky man in a fur coat, reached out his leg to give the creature a swift kick. Kindhearted Ethan was noticing and gave the fellow a nudge to knock him off his balance and spare the animal a crippling injury.

In an instant, the tall man spun around, discarded his gloves, and roared, "The glubs er off!" His slurred speech left a spear of frost in front of his ruddy face. The accent sounded not quite English, Irish, or Canadian. I wondered if he was a Scot. The crowd moving along the boardwalk—prospectors and hired men from the creeks, doctors, lawyers, gamblers, bankers, dance-hall girls, actresses, shopkeepers, and clerks—fell back in a loose circle, anticipating a fight.

One of the drunk's companions, a peacock of a fellow in a double-breasted Prince Albert coat with a diamond stickpin, retrieved the gloves with his silver cane and was handed the long fur coat. His full dark beard struck me as an unlikely match with his bowler hat, high button boots, and all the rest. Most likely he was a gambler, though gamblers tended to sport goatees or go clean-shaven. It was working men and the prospectors out at the creeks who favored full beards.

The would-be dog kicker, meanwhile, was circling Ethan in a boxer's stance with fists held high. His graying, waxed handlebar mustache extended far past his face. The shape of his head brought to mind a thin slab of chiseled granite. His nose was anything but angular, squashed flat as if by a streetcar.

"I apologize," Ethan said sincerely. "I was afraid the dog would get hurt."

"S'what?" the tall man retorted, redder-faced than before. "He belongs in the street, not on the boardwalk. Is the cur yers?"

"No, he's not."

The drunk looked around. "Anybody's?"

No one answered. All the while, the dog was watching closely. Its eyes went from one of them to the other and back. Its thin ears, when Ethan was talking, stood straight up. When the drunk spoke, their top halves folded forward, as if on hinges.

"I didn't think so. Well, then, mate . . ."

Quick as a cobra, the tall man's long arm flicked out. The speed of it was surprising from a man who could have been forty and was three sheets to the wind. Barely in time, Ethan rolled his jaw to the side and took the punch glancingly. I saw the alarm and anger in Abraham's eyes. Though Abraham walked with a limp, he was nearly as tall as this boxer, strong as whipcord, and fiercely protective of his brothers.

Ethan raised his hands calmly to protest, but the man continued in his fighting crouch, hands in motion. It was then I noticed Irish Nellie Cashman pushing her way to the front of the crowd.

Distracted by Irish Nellie, Ethan took a sudden punch in the stomach.

"Deal with the bully, Ethan!" Irish Nellie cried.

Recognizing the tiny woman, Ethan was amused by her eagerness for him to mix it up. The day before, Irish

Nellie had come to the sawmill for a donation to the home she wanted to build for the downtrodden, just like the one she told about building in Tombstone, Arizona.

"Careful," Abe whispered. Ethan was no fighter.

"Don't, Hawthorn," someone yelled from the crowd. "That's the Sydney Mauler!"

We hadn't heard the name before, but we got the picture.

In an instant, the Sydney Mauler, with a darting left, drew blood from Ethan's nose. Ethan removed his mittens and handed them to me. My brother wiped his hand across his face, saw the bright crimson there. His broad forehead furrowed with determination. It did the same at the mill when he was wrestling logs or huge pieces of machinery.

His long-armed opponent was in a fighter's crouch, but not for long. With a quick right hand, Ethan put him on the icy ground. The boxer got to his knees with his eyes still swimming, then fell back on his hindquarters, supporting himself with one hand. He stared at Ethan with surprise and anger. Then a grin spread slowly across his face.

The crowd erupted. "Well struck, Ethan," Irish Nellie rejoiced. A grizzled miner held Ethan's right hand aloft. Taken aback, Ethan wrenched his hand down.

"Don't you know who the Sydney Mauler is?" The voice had come from the peacock with the dark beard.

Ethan shrugged, shook his head. The drunk, having regained his feet, was reaching for his coat and gloves.

"This gentleman is none other than Henry Brackett of Sydney, Australia, alias the Sydney Mauler, former heavyweight champion of the British Empire!"

Ethan looked at the boxer, then back to his cohort with the silver cane. "And who are you?"

With a short, theatrical bow, he introduced himself as "Cornelius Donner, promoter *extraordinaire*."

With his dark, piercing eyes fastened on Ethan, the promoter reached out and shook his hand. In a friendly, soothing baritone, he said, "I'm pleased to make your acquaintance. Hawthorn's your name?"

Ethan was one to make friends quickly, but I watched him catch himself. "I've got to get back to the mill. If you'll excuse me, let's all get out of the cold."

"We'll meet again," the boxer growled. "And not when I'm half-seas over."

"Rematch!" someone yelled.

"*Grudge* match!" declared the promoter, smiling like a rogue.

"Rematch!" the crowd roared. "Grudge match!"

Ethan was shaking his head. "Let's get back to work, Jason. Enough with this foolishness."

"Amen to that," Abraham agreed.

We headed up Front Street toward the sawmill. Just before we angled out of sight, I looked back where we'd been. Still abuzz, the crowd hadn't dispersed.

That's when I heard the pat of small feet and looked down to see that split-faced black mutt close on Ethan's heels. "Look behind you, Ethan," I said. "You better run Nuisance off while you have the chance. He'll stick to you like glue."

Ethan reached down to pet the beggar on the head. "We got anything to feed him at the mill? Should I take him to the cabin?"

Now I understood how that creature had made it over the Chilkoot Pass and five hundred miles down the Yukon.

TWO

"I believe she's cooked, Jason."

Same time every morning, I waited for Ethan to say those magic words. It was coffee he was talking about, boiling away on the Yukon stove. Next, Abe would make a remark about Ethan leaving it on the stove too long.

"Likely you've rendered that brew into cyanide," Abe said dryly as he worried his mustache. "We can sell the grounds to the fellows out at the creeks for separating gold."

Ethan laughed heartily. "Don't you throw 'em out before I've had the chance to chew 'em, Abraham."

I laughed as I pulled on a leather mitt and grabbed the big coffee pot by the handle. I stepped outside the mill office by the light of our new electric yard lamp into the subzero cold and whirled the pot high over my head and nearly to my feet, around and around in a blur until the grounds were good and settled. Abe held that sinking the grounds with a cup of cold water was more effective, not to mention safer. It was Ethan, impish by nature, who'd taught me how to windmill the coffee. He never failed to watch through the partly frosted windows. In the never-ending seesaw between my older brothers, Ethan got to win out on the small things.

I brought the coffee back inside, shucked the mitt, and poured three cups. I held mine for a few minutes to warm my hands. This was my favorite ritual, this half hour before the crew showed up, when it was just the brothers Hawthorn starting the workday with coffee and the newspaper and conversation.

"That Sydney Mauler," I said. "Imagine, Ethan—heavyweight champion of the British Empire."

"Former champion," Abe pointed out as he read the front page of the *Klondike Nugget.*

Ethan chuckled and waved it off, spitting a few coffee grounds through his teeth onto the floor. "It was all a tempest in a teapot."

"You wouldn't get into the ring with him, would you?" I asked.

Abe put the newspaper down. He was cross. "Of course he wouldn't."

I looked at Ethan. As preposterous as it sounded, he seemed to be amused by the idea. Now that Abe had opposed it, Ethan would have to consider it. Lately that's the way it was between the two of them.

I heard a loud thump outside. "What was that?"

"Something thrown at the fence?" Abraham guessed.

Sipping my coffee, I got up and walked to the window. "Nothing out there."

Suddenly there *was* something there. Running full speed at the wooden fence around the lumberyard, here came that little split-faced mongrel from the night before, ears flapping. With a sudden leap, as if he meant to clear the fence, the mutt bounded skyward. The thing was, that fence was six feet high if it was an inch. The dog crashed with a heavy thump and fell to the ground. I couldn't help laughing.

The mutt picked himself up, trotted off a few feet and studied the top of the fence again. His head was cocked sideways as if his eyesight were better out of the blue eye.

"Take a look at this," I said. "You're not going to believe it. He's going to try again."

Abe and Ethan joined me at the window as the mongrel was making its third attempt, this time from across the street. "Well, I'll be," Ethan said, pulling on his curly beard.

The dog had built up terrific speed. I had to admire his determination, though he had a bird's nest for brains.

Like Jules Verne's rocket to the moon, the mutt went airborne, so high he was clawing for a grip on the top rail. For a second he hung there like a monkey. Then, more like a cat, he pulled himself up and onto the rail, which was nothing but a two-by-four.

The mongrel trotted toward us along the top of the fence—he had us spotted inside the office—and jumped down when he got to the gate.

Ethan whistled and said, "Darnedest thing I ever saw."

Shortly came a scratch at the office door.

"It's for you, Ethan," I said. "Told you he'd stick like glue once you fed him. I saw him outside the cabin this morning."

"Did I hear you shooing him away?"

"Trying to. Looks like he didn't go far."

Ethan went to the door, and there stood that shivering mongrel with its half-black, half-white face and the strange blue eye, and the hinged ears. A second later he was in Ethan's lap and Ethan was resting his coffee cup on the dog's skinny rump. "Look, he likes it," Ethan said. "Coffee's warming him up. Wonder if I gave him some, if he'd drink it."

I was shaking my head.

Ethan looked at me funny. "I don't fathom you, Jason. How could you not like this little feller? You, of all people. I know how you are."

"Because he's useless," I said. "Got no business in the North. A dog up here should be good for something."

Both my brothers were thinking it over. They'd never laid eyes on King. They never saw the two of us climbing the Chilkoot, time after time, both loaded down like pack mules.

Thoughts of King sent me into a reverie. Suddenly I could see the husky's amber eyes, the sweep of the great tail across his back, his claws digging into the ice as he pulled the heavily loaded canoe over skid logs on the portage trails. Now, *that* was a dog.

Of course I wasn't being fair to the mutt. He couldn't help being useless. Somebody must have brought him here for a pet and then abandoned him. It wasn't like I was going to go out of my way to be cruel to him. I just didn't much care for him, and wished Ethan wouldn't get started with him.

As Ethan gently stroked the mutt's head, the dog closed its eyes contentedly. Ethan was already hooked.

The next morning, Nuisance followed us through the gate. I would rather have seen him scale the fence again. It didn't take him long to find his way back onto Ethan's lap.

"I hear thirty-five thousand men are working on the railroad over the White Pass," Ethan said as he broke off a corner of hard biscuit and fed it to the dog, who took it with his rubbery black lips instead of his teeth. "They say it'll reach Lake Bennett this summer. Imagine not having to deal with White Pass or the Chilkoot the hard way."

"Don't talk to me about the hard way," I joked. "You guys had pack horses."

Ethan laughed, slapped himself on the thigh. Startled for the moment, the dog lifted its ears straight up. Ethan stroked the crown of the mutt's head reassuringly. "But you like doing things the hard way, Jason. Surprises me that city life suits you after all your time in the bush."

"It's so big out there. So many stars, and free as free can get so long as you don't starve. Someday I suppose I *will* go back to the wilderness."

"It's never far away," Abe commented. "It's all around us like a vast ocean. I never cease to be amazed at all the activity in our little metropolis in the bush, thousands of miles from civilization. Three years ago Dawson was a swamp, and now it not only has electricity, it's got running water and hot-water heat—practically everything but the telegraph."

"People say our hotels are furnished as fancy as any in New York," Ethan added appreciatively. "Not that I'd know. Jason, you've been there."

"Where I stayed, it wasn't the Waldorf."

"What about some of these fancy restaurants here in Dawson? We should rent tailcoats sometime, Abraham . . . go to one of those places with the string orchestras . . . order pâté de foie gras. What do you say?"

Abe's disapproving eyebrow rose, as Ethan knew it would, and Abe said, as I knew he would, "You don't even know what pâté de foie gras is, Ethan. I sure don't."

"Exactly," Ethan replied a little testily. "I don't have the slightest idea. That's why we should order it. Just for a lark, Abe."

I glanced at Abe. He didn't think this was amusing. For Abe, a lark was a bird. That's the only kind of lark he knew.

To steer them away from each other, I put in, "I wonder how Nome will affect us."

"Gold in the beach sand?" Abe scoffed. "I don't believe it. The news is garbled as can be. At any rate, Nome is seventeen hundred miles away."

The dog was back on four legs, about to launch himself into *my* lap. I didn't stop him. Once there, he rolled partway over. I gathered my thoughts as I rested my warm coffee cup on his pink belly. He rolled his eyes at me in an ecstasy of comfort. Ethan chuckled softly.

"The news is garbled only because it was conveyed by a series of dog teams," I maintained. "People retold it along the way. By all accounts it happened last fall. Three lucky Swedes, they say. Gold in the beach sand and nuggets in the creeks. I believe it."

Abe pulled at his mustache. "For argument's sake, let's suppose that it's true. If Nome affects us it will only be to draw off some of these men milling up and down Front Street looking for excitement."

Ethan was irked. "There's not enough work to go around. You know that, Abraham. Anyway, who's to blame those men for living for today? I agree with them—worry about tomorrow when it comes."

Through the window, I could see our crew approaching the gate. I gulped a last swallow of coffee, glanced at my brothers, and stole the line that was usually Abe's: "Let's make some lumber, gentlemen."

THREE

Ethan may have been itching to join the excitement of Front Street, but so far the Hawthorn brothers knew merely secondhand of Dawson's celebrated goings-on. We were busy making lumber. We'd hear and read about the personalities—the kings of the Klondike like Big Alex McDonald and Swiftwater Bill Gates; the lucky owners of tiny fractional claims like whip-cracking Dick Lowe; famous gamblers like Silent Sam Bonnifield and Louis Golden; and the dance-hall queens like Cad Wilson and Diamond Tooth Gertie.

Buckskin Frank Leslie was said to be in town, a famous gunman from frontier days, and so was Calamity Jane, whose name was linked to Wild Bill Hickok and Deadwood, South Dakota. Arizona Charlie Meadows of the Palace Grand was a former cavalry scout who was said to have once fought hand-to-hand with Geronimo. Jack Dalton was celebrated in Dawson for blazing his own trail from tidewater to the Yukon below Five Fingers Rapids. Driving two thousand cattle this far north, to a town desperate for anything other than bacon and beans and flapjacks, was a near-impossible and instantly legendary feat.

I'd heard hundreds of nicknames, like Limejoice Lil, Spanish Dolores, Deep-Hole Johnson, Two-Step Louie, Hamgrease Jimmy, and the Evaporated Kid. Sometimes I'd heard the story behind the name. Spare-rib Jimmy Mackinson was so thin that his landlady wouldn't let him sleep in her sheets for fear he'd tear them with his ribs. Waterfront Brown was the name of the infamous bill collector who haunted the riverfront during the summer season. That's when people running off on their debts were likely to try to board the steamboats.

Dawson was a town that loved its personalities so much, it manufactured new ones overnight. Little did we know that the next would be one of the Hawthorn brothers. When an article under the headline GRUDGE MATCH appeared in the *Klondike Nugget* three days after Ethan's incident with the Sydney Mauler, we were taken by surprise.

"'A new heavyweight opponent for Henry Brackett, known as the Sydney Mauler, looms large,'" I read aloud. My voice was short of breath.

"Go on," Ethan said, poking at the mill ends firing our small Yukon stove. It was an especially cold morning, with frost still clinging to the windows despite our fire.

"'The opponent's name, as dubbed by Brackett, is "Lucky Ethan" Hawthorn. All of Dawson is talking about the fight.'"

Abe frowned. "It wasn't before, but I'm sure it will be now."

"Go on," Ethan urged, his impish green eyes sparkling. "Keep reading."

"'Little did a local man know Saturday afternoon that in his street brawl in defense of one of Dawson's innumerable homeless canines, he had bested the pride of Sydney, Australia, whom two great heavyweight champions of the world, John L. Sullivan and Gentleman Jim Corbett, have dodged in trepidation of his pugilistic prowess.'"

With a snort, Abe remarked, "This newspaper uses a pound of butter to lather a morsel of bread. My guess is, Brackett couldn't get a title fight because he's moldy cheese in the fight game. Why else would he be here?"

"Is that the end of the article?" Ethan asked.

"Not quite," I replied, amused by Ethan's excitement and Abe's annoyance. "Listen to this: 'Will "Lucky Ethan," the ox-strong co-owner with his brothers of Dawson's own Hawthorn Brothers Sawmill, take up the gauntlet thrown down during Saturday's street brawl?'"

"Rubbish," Abe said, and reached across for the newspaper. He tried to snatch it out of my hands, but Ethan grabbed it first.

"'According to observers, the Brackett–Hawthorn grudge match is a near certainty,'" Ethan continued.

"What observers?" Abe erupted. "The papers are obviously in league with that promoter with the silver cane, whatever his name was. These so-called 'grudge matches' are a dime a dozen. When we came across Brackett and his promoter, those two were undoubtedly out looking for a new chicken to pluck, and you're the ch—"

"Donner was the promoter's name," Ethan said. "Cornelius Donner."

I couldn't resist. "I do believe you're interested in this grudge match, Ethan."

"Stop it," Abe ordered. "Jason, a professional fighter would tear your brother to ribbons."

Ethan just laughed and headed out the door to work.

The men at the mill already knew about the newspaper story. It made for a strange day. Nobody was really concentrating on what they were doing, me included and Ethan especially. Abe was stewing. You could lose fingers or a hand or your life for lack of concentration at the mill.

There were dozens of reporters in Dawson City, not only for the *Nugget* but for newspapers and magazines all across the continent and even Europe. By afternoon five newshounds were at the sawmill wanting statements from Ethan. The next day it was a large pack—Ethan had become an overnight sensation. Abraham kept trying to shoo them away, but Ethan was enjoying the attention. For several days he told them there wasn't going to be a fight; then suddenly he announced, "Only if the proceeds go to the home that Irish Nellie's trying to build."

Now the newspapers had something to trumpet, and it went straight to the headlines. Before long, and much to Abe's dismay, Ethan was negotiating with the peacock with the Prince Albert coat and the piercing eyes, Cornelius Donner.

Here's the deal Ethan struck: If Henry Brackett won, two-thirds of the proceeds would go to Donner and Brackett and one-third to Irish Nellie's home for the downtrodden. But if Ethan won, the entire proceeds would go to Nellie.

"You're going to get your brains stove in," Abe told Ethan.

With a broad grin, Ethan replied, "In a good cause."

Because Ethan was going to fight for charity, there was nothing more Abe could say. Resigned to the fight, Abe rented time in the gym for the three weeks remaining before the match, then found a boxing coach for Ethan. He also found four sparring heavyweights with ring experience. One was Joe Boyle, Brackett's Canadian sparring partner. Abe wasn't going to let his brother get into the ring with the former heavyweight champion of the British Empire and be bludgeoned to ground meat if he could help it. Boyle told the *Nugget* that Ethan was learning faster than anyone he ever saw. Abe said it was a lie intended to whip up interest in the fight.

During those three weeks, Ethan and his mutt, who was always at his side, became the talk of Dawson City. Hundreds came to watch his sparring sessions and debate his chances. After a few weeks, Ethan started to look convincing. He'd always looked determined. Everyone in town wanted him to win. Everybody had to pat the mutt on the head "for good luck." When first asked the mongrel's name, Ethan thought for a second and then said, "Underdog. But Jason, my little brother here, calls him Nuisance."

The reporters were writing all this down. While scribbling, one said, "You call him Underdog because *you're* the underdog?"

"No, because he's always underfoot. We can't move around the cabin or the mill without stepping on his toes."

True, I thought.

There was laughter all around. Ethan had an easygoing way with people and an honest face. He could sense that he was loved, and he loved being a personality.

"None of it means a thing if I don't win," Ethan told me confidentially. "Nobody will remember my name the next day unless I win."

"You mean to win? It's not just what you're telling the papers?"

I saw those furrows gather in his forehead as deep as I'd ever seen them. "I aim to win," he replied.

"Does Brackett's sparring partner really think you're good?"

"He says I'm good enough to have a chance."

Abe didn't like it that I'd leave the mill for an hour or so every day to see Ethan train, but he had the good sense not to forbid me—I'd have gone anyway. The atmosphere at the gym was electric, and I was getting an eyeful and an earful of Dawson's quirky personalities.

On a Thursday, the crowd stampeded out of the gym when word came that One-Eyed Riley had a winning streak going down at the Monte Carlo. I'd never heard of One-Eyed Riley, but I ran along to see what it was all about. Riley, people were saying, worked nights as a watchman at one of the warehouses and spent the day-time hours gambling, which wasn't unusual. Nearly everyone in Dawson but the Hawthorn brothers, it seemed, was burning the candle at both ends.

The story was that Riley, until this streak, had always been a loser at the faro tables. But this time it was different. From the Monte Carlo to the Pavilion to the Palace Grand, Riley kept betting the limit and kept winning. It was hard to squirm far enough through the crowd to catch a glimpse of him at the tables, but I managed. When Riley left the Palace Grand and marched at the head of the crowd toward the Tivoli, I broke off and headed for the mill.

I was sure Riley's luck couldn't last for long, but

lo and behold, the streak was still going the next morning. More than a thousand onlookers were following One-Eyed Riley up and down the street. I couldn't help tagging along.

It looked as if Riley couldn't lose. People were making a lot of money by making side bets on his cards. The side betting was still raging when a rumor started to circulate that the fellow now dealing to Riley was a cardsharp hired by the Monte Carlo.

Riley couldn't have heard the rumor, but he was spooked anyway. Something about the man across the table had scared him, and scared him bad. "I quit," he announced, and yelled out, "Somebody get me the best musher in town—I'm going south today. If I stay, I know I can't stop."

Within hours, Riley and his fortune were bundled in a dogsled and heading for the Chilkoot Pass, five hundred miles away.

Just before he left Dawson, One-Eyed Riley stopped in at the gym. The fight was two days away. He kissed Nuisance on the lips—for good luck, he explained. Raising Ethan's hand high, Riley proclaimed, "The underdog by a knockout! If I was a gambling man, I'd put all my money on Hawthorn!"

There was nervous laughter all around the gym. Nobody in Ethan's own camp believed he had a chance.

Finally the night for the fight arrived. It was the last day of March, and the location was the Palace Grand. The ring was on the exact same stage where Jamie had recited her father's poems of the rush, to packed houses drunk on sentiment.

This time the crowd was drunk on whiskey. Its sweet reek pervaded the theater, and so did cigar smoke thick as ground fog. The seats had sold for fifty dollars, twice the usual. Diamond stickpin glittering, Cornelius Donner introduced the fighters and said something about ten rounds, though nobody in the house, including me, thought Ethan could last more than one or two.

Everyone was wrong. My huge-hearted brother wouldn't go down, no matter that he was taking a fearsome beating. His legs, veterans of all his years of heavy labor, refused to buckle, though his face was slashed and bruised and his right eye had swollen shut.

The former heavyweight champion of the British Empire was anything but unscathed. Brackett's granite features had turned to ruddy clay. Gone were the sneer and the haughty look of superiority with which the tall fighter had stepped into the ring.

In the fifth round, to the surprise of the crowd, Ethan sent the Sydney Mauler to one knee. The crowd responded with a tumultuous roar that seemed to give Ethan fresh strength. I couldn't fathom how he even lifted his arms.

All the while the mutt was barking at Henry Brackett—not that anyone could hear.

By the eighth round I swore to myself that I'd never attend another prizefight so long as I lived. I prayed that my brother would live through this. At my side, Abe looked like he had his doubts.

In the ninth round both fighters were barely able to stand on their feet, and few blows were landed.

In the tenth, bedlam erupted as the crowd clamored for a resolution. It would be impossible, the way the two had fought, for the judges to decide a winner on points.

Brackett, with a long left arm, knocked my burly brother down for the first time.

It took until the count of six for Ethan to regain his feet. Abraham reached for the towel to throw it into the ring. Someone from behind snatched it away from him and the fight continued.

Brackett began throwing punches like a windmill, but too wildly to connect. I noticed Ethan studying him, biding his time. Then Ethan, with a single right hand, connected with everything he had.

The Sydney Mauler went down like falling timber.

The next day, ground was broken for Irish Nellie's boardinghouse for the downtrodden.

Ethan wasn't the same after that. I don't know if it was all the blows to the head, or too much attention, or a combination of both. He wasn't the same.

FOUR

After the fight, Ethan had as many friends as a dog has fleas. He didn't come to work at the mill much, and when he did, he'd tell the men of his personal acquaintance with the glittering personalities of the Golden City, including the kings of the Klondike. One night at the Monte Carlo, none other than Swiftwater Bill Gates had handed him a fancy cigar and lit it with a fifty-dollar bill. Big Alex McDonald gave a banquet for him where sixty-dollar champagne flowed like water and pâté de foie gras was served. "That's goose livers!" Ethan told the men. "Chopped goose livers!"

The newspaper called him by the name Brackett had prophetically bestowed on him. There was a story about Lucky Ethan cutting the ribbon for the opening of Irish Nellie's boardinghouse in the block behind the Northern. I read it to Abraham one evening after work. Nellie had a new nickname—"the miner's angel."

Ethan rarely came home anymore, whether due to his success or to Abraham's disapproval it was hard to tell. I got to a part of the newspaper story that told of Ethan making appearances at all the dance halls along Front Street and the famous personalities he'd danced with, including Diamond Tooth Gertie, Caprice, Ping Pong, and Cad Wilson. It began to tell of a photograph that had been taken of Ethan and Cad Wilson, with Nuisance curled up on the redhead's lap.

"Stop," Abraham said softly. "Don't read me any more of that racy rubbage, Jason." Abe sounded eighty years old.

"You don't understand," I said. "The dance-hall girls may be colorful, but they're respectable. The dancing is as proper as can be. Everyone at the mill says so."

Abraham raised an eyebrow. "As I understand it, they dance to collect tokens, which cost a dollar. They get to keep a quarter. Is this a respectable way to make a living? All the while, they're encouraging the men to buy drinks. It's a scheme by the ownership to sell liquor."

I hesitated. "I don't suppose there's anything wrong in all of that. . . ."

"No?" Abe sighed and looked back at me, holding his eyes on mine. Then he said, "Do you mean to say you've paid them to dance with you?"

"I haven't," I said truthfully.

"Why not, then, if there's nothing wrong in it? Too shy, are you?"

For a moment I hated Abraham's self-righteousness. I had an idea it was part of what was keeping Ethan away. "That's not it," I insisted.

"What is it, then?"

"Because of Jamie, I suppose."

My oldest brother nodded his approval. "Good for

you, then. I hope she does come back, Jason. It's not so far off—the first boat up the river should arrive in early June."

"I know," I said. In fact, I was counting the days.

"But Jason, you have to allow that Jamie and her father have been on a tour all across the continent. They've been treated like royalty wherever they go. . . . Remember, she's the Princess of Dawson."

"I know, I know."

"You've seen, on a *smaller* scale, what fame can do to a person."

"Jamie won't get too big for her britches, Abraham."

Abe smiled at my choice of words. "You'll find out soon if they still fit . . . if she comes back."

I stood up, turned my back on him. His last "if" had me boiling. "I'm going out," I said without explanation.

I wandered down to Front Street looking for Ethan. Tracking him down didn't take long; everybody in town knew Ethan by now. I found him in Silent Sam Bonnifield's Bank Saloon and Gambling House at the corner of Front and King, across from the Alaska Commercial Store. Ethan was watching Silent Sam gamble with a fellow whose face I couldn't make out from where I stood. Raptly observing the master, Ethan didn't notice me as I came in.

Nuisance noticed, however, and wagged that bent tail at the sight of me. I was allowed to gradually weave my way through the crowd—people recognized me as Ethan's brother—until I stood at Ethan's shoulder, which I gave a pat. He looked back, saw me there, and gave me that golden smile of his. "Jason," he whispered. Nothing had soured between the two of us, at least.

The room was in a profound hush. My eyes went to the pot on the poker table and I understood why. There was an enormous amount of cash there.

Silent Sam was also called Square Sam because he ran an honest game. The man across the table was Louis Golden, also called Goldie. It turned out that this was a weekly game. The two were the owners of rival establishments, which they would close on alternating weeks to match wits and luck.

Bonnifield was in his early thirties, slender and handsome, as taciturn as a marble statue. His blue eyes lacked any hint of expression. Golden, on the other hand, didn't seem to mind sharing his ups and downs with the onlookers.

There was fifty thousand dollars in the pot when Goldie confidently raised Silent Sam by twenty-five thousand. The crowd gasped at the enormity of the stakes. They all knew what money was worth, and so did I. Back in Seattle, in the years after our father died, my brothers and I shared a three-room apartment that cost five dollars a month. Back then I worked at a cannery for ten cents an hour, ten hours a day. It was the going wage in the States, and if wages had improved in the several years since, it couldn't have been by more than a couple cents.

Silent Sam called Golden and raised him. There was now $150,000 in that pot.

Goldie in turn called him and raised him. He had a smile playing at his lips.

This time Bonnifield was content to call.

With a triumphant flourish, Goldie laid down four queens.

Silent Sam, with no expression whatsoever, laid down four kings. His long arm reached across the table and raked in a fortune.

• • •

The next time I went looking for Ethan I found him at the Bodega Saloon. This time Ethan wasn't looking on. He was gambling, though not with large amounts, and he was winning more than he was losing. To my surprise, Cornelius Donner came and went from the table, and the two of them seemed fast friends.

In fact, I was astounded. To me the warmth in Donner's voice sounded no more genuine than his costume. When Donner looked at me out of the corner of his penetrating eyes—he never addressed me—I saw nothing in them but the depths and darkness of a bottomless well.

When I caught Ethan alone I alluded to his gambling money by kidding that he must have turned prospector and discovered a new gold creek. He told me that Donner was the owner of the saloon and had staked him.

I wondered why Donner would give Ethan money. I guessed it was a way of trying to bribe Ethan into more boxing matches, even though Ethan had told everyone in town he'd never fight again.

In the days to come, now that Ethan had a cash grubstake, he turned in earnest to playing the fool on fortune's wheel. Roulette, poker, faro, three-card monte, he played them all, not only at the Bodega but all up and down Front Street, and at midnight he went dancing. One night Abe sent me to try to bring him home, but Lucky Ethan was winning. He assured me that he was "really living" for the first time in his life. "Tell Abraham . . . ," he declared, and then Ethan couldn't come up with the words. He'd been drinking and he couldn't think straight. "Why even bother?" he said finally.

The rest of April there was alcohol on Ethan's breath. He no longer checked in at the mill.

"I've lost him," Abe lamented.

So had I.

The trouble was, Ethan kept winning. Not all the time, but often enough for his nickname to seem deserved. Still, "lucky" isn't the word I would have used to describe him.

There were storm warnings wherever Ethan might have looked, but he wasn't looking. All Dawson was talking about another gambler, a nattily dressed man who waltzed into the Northern, directly to the roulette wheel, and laid a thousand dollars on the red. The wheel stopped on black. He bet another thousand on the red, and lost again. Stolidly, he bet on the red a third time, laying another thousand on the felt. Again, it went to the house.

Like a mule butting its bloodied head against its stall, the man bet seven more times on the red, and lost every time.

Finally, showing no emotion, the man walked away. At the bar, he ordered a drink. The next day the newspaper reported that he said to the bartender, "I went broke." With that, he walked into the street and shot himself in the head.

Another man who'd lost everything stayed drunk and raved that a huge black python was after him.

Ethan must have heard about these two, and others. He couldn't quit.

I questioned my long infatuation with the Golden City. A madness had infected the San Francisco of the North, and it had ahold of my brother.

One night I heard he might be at the Opera House attending a vaudeville show, and I set out to find him. Amid a sea of men on the ground floor I tracked him by his hearty laugh to one of the private boxes above, where he was applauding lustily, gulping champagne, and peeling off bills for the waiter. Cornelius Donner was in the box, Henry Brackett too—all three were in tailcoats. They were surrounded by a bevy of dance-hall girls with heavy nugget chains around their waists.

I caught Ethan as he was leaving the theater, pulled him away from his friends, and spoke my mind. In fact I poured my heart out. My brother was so drunk he could barely keep on his feet, but he listened, wide-eyed. At the last, I appealed to the memory of our father, who used to call drinking and gambling "the engines of calamity."

After a long silence, Ethan said, "Abraham sent you."

I shook my head. "No, Ethan, this is me."

He went his way, I went mine. I found out the next day that I'd been talking to the owner of a half-interest in a dance hall—the Monte Carlo, no less—and a third share of Forty Above, a fabulously rich claim on Eldorado Creek. Ethan had been winning big. Suddenly he was, if not one of the kings of the Klondike, one of its dukes or earls. Compared to his present station, part ownership of a sawmill was a penny-ante game.

Dawson City–style, everything kept happening fast. Within days, the men at the mill were saying that Ethan's luck had turned—he was on a losing streak. I worried that he'd be ruined. An old hand at the mill told me, "He can lose feathers and still fly. It depends on how many get pulled out."

Loss was in the air. From the *Nugget*, Abraham read to me of the passing of Joseph Ladue. The founder of Dawson City was the man who'd set us up in business and granted us 51-percent ownership of the sawmill. He died far from the Klondike, of tuberculosis, at his Adirondacks farm in New York State. After thirteen years of hardship in the North, he'd finally struck it rich by claiming forty acres of swamp where the Klondike meets the Yukon. A day or two after George Washington Carmack's fabulous discovery, Ladue guessed right that a town would rise there.

"*Sic transit gloria*," Abraham commented. "Joseph Ladue was one of the most famous men in the country when he died. Worth five million dollars, they say, and now the worms are making supper of him."

"Don't be so gloomy," I said. I knew Abe was thinking more of Ethan than Joseph Ladue.

"At least he was able to live a year or so after he returned triumphant. It says he married his long-suffering sweetheart."

FIVE

Maybe it was Abraham saying "sweetheart" that set my heart on edge. I went to the Palace Grand to see Arizona Charlie Meadows. I had to find out if he'd heard anything from Jamie's father regarding their return to Dawson City.

When Jamie and her father left in July, Arizona Charlie had promised them their place in his show for the following summer. Jamie's performances of her father's Klondike poetry, with Homer scribbling in the background against the backdrop of a log cabin, had never failed to pack the house. Yet before '98 was out, Meadows had invented a new act featuring Little Margie Newman, shamelessly billing her as the Princess of the Klondike.

I'd been certain that Jamie and Homer's loyal audiences at the Palace Grand would turn a cold shoulder to the new act, but I was dead wrong. In the place of Jamie performing her father's authentic narratives of the rush, Meadows gave the audiences a nine-year-old singing songs so sentimental they were nauseating.

To my dismay, the same townsmen and the same grizzled men from the creeks who'd showered Jamie with wildflowers not only bestowed the pretender with their affection, they tossed nuggets onto the stage until Little Margie was heel-deep in them while blowing her kisses. All this for a nine-year-old as authentic to the North as a flamingo.

Jamie, on the other hand, had been born and raised in the North, in the bush no less. Until the age of twelve she lived at Fort Chipewyan, the Hudson Bay Company's outpost way up on Lake Athabaska. Homer was a trader working with the Indians in those days.

Arizona Charlie Meadows knew me on sight as Jamie's friend. The famous marksman greeted me at his office door with a somber expression. I assumed it was because he was about to tell me what I already expected, that the Princess of the Klondike and the Princess of Dawson couldn't perform on the same stage.

"Sit down, sit down," the man in buckskins said with a deep, reverberating voice like far-off thunder. He took off his wide-brimmed hat, bowed his silver head, and said, "I have tragic news."

My God, I thought, she's dead.

Numb, I sank into the gilded chair he offered. Arizona Charlie looked out the window onto the frozen Yukon. Without turning to speak, he said at last, "I learned only days ago—a dog team got through from Skagway with the mails—that the poet has passed away."

"The poet?" I repeated. For a moment I couldn't think who in the world he was talking about.

Then, of course, I knew. "You don't mean Homer. . . ."

"I do indeed. His heart suddenly failed him. In Philadelphia, they say."

"What about Jamie?"

The frontiersman's eyes met mine. "I know nothing of her. I'm sorry. Nothing was mentioned of Jamie."

Arizona Charlie paused, then seated himself behind his desk. "Jamie is an extraordinary talent. I'm sure she'll find work on the stage. Doubtless she's already been flooded with offers. Don't worry about her having plenty of friends and theater people to look out for her."

"But she'll come back here," I heard myself saying aloud.

Arizona Charlie looked at me and shrugged. "All the way to the ends of the earth? I wouldn't think so."

I went mute, stunned as if he'd hit me with a fish club. I felt sorry for myself, but a minute later, walking away, it hit me all over again and I came to my senses. I felt sorry for Jamie.

At that very time, Ethan was in the midst of a colossal gambling binge. He'd lost his share in the Monte Carlo and was on his way to losing his piece of the claim on Eldorado Creek. My brother was a runaway train. He couldn't stop whether he was winning *or* losing.

Abraham knew all this was going on, but he couldn't bear to hear about it. Anyway, he was busy trying to get Dawson City's fire department back to work. Abe was the head of a citizen's group fighting for higher wages for the firemen, who had been on strike since the first week of April. Dawson City was in jeopardy every single day they were on strike, as everyone in town, including the town council, knew full well. The department of a hundred men had been formed after the disastrous Thanksgiving fire only five months before.

Half a million dollars in real estate had burned on Thanksgiving Day in a quick conflagration, and all that could be done to stop the blaze was to tear down businesses and cabins that were in its way. A fire in the spring of '99 would be far more disastrous, Abraham pleaded to the council, but the council stood firm.

The firemen retaliated by letting the fires under their boilers go out.

Ethan's last hand was dealt sometime during the evening of April 25. In all likelihood he hadn't slept in several days. It was Silent Sam Bonnifield who cleaned him out, I learned the next morning from the men at the mill. Ever since Ethan had started gambling for high stakes, I'd stayed away. I didn't have the stomach for it. A thousand times afterward, I wished I'd sought him out, given his addled brain a good swipe with a lead pipe, and dragged him home. I should've handcuffed him to his bed.

After Ethan was cleaned out, he started on a drinking spree. When fire broke out the next night, April 26, on the second floor of the Bodega Saloon, Ethan had been unaccounted for since the wee hours of the morning; I'd been scouring the town all day trying to find him and bring him home. Abe and I figured that his madness would be spent now that he'd hit rock bottom.

I was there on Front Street when flames erupted from the second floor of the Bodega. It was bitter cold, around forty-five degrees below zero. Everyone on the street, including me, started yelling "Fire!" A moment later dozens of people burst from the saloon into the cold, including Cornelius Donner, for once without his Prince Albert coat. Donner hollered, "Fire! Fire! My saloon! For God's sake, someone rouse the fire department!"

Just that quick, the second stories of the adjoining buildings were ablaze, too. With the night sky glowing at my back like an aurora, I raced to our cabin on the hillside to alert Abe. As I burst inside, he'd just heard the alarm bells and had come to the window. By now there was a parade of flame along the tops of a good many of the false fronts of Front Street. "Oh my God," Abe muttered. "Oh my God." He was thinking fast. "They'll need dry lumber," he declared, and began to snatch up his clothes.

"Dry lumber?" I repeated incredulously.

"Hand me my boots—no time to explain!"

We ran to the mill, hitched up the team, and raced a load of dry scrap as close to the fire as the terrified horses would allow. As Abe had foreseen, men were down on the ice on the river, trying to melt the spot the fire department had formerly counted on for their emergency water supply. Before the strike, the spot had always been kept open, but April 26 found it frozen several feet thick. Men with axes had raced to the river to chop it open, but men with axes were no match for the speed of the inferno overtaking the city.

I struggled up the bank with a firehose for one of the pumps parked on Front Street. I was standing only ten yards from the British Bank of North America, which was all ablaze, and I barely felt the heat, so intense was the extreme cold.

Abe and the men at the river burned their way to running water. The pumps were started at last. But as the hoses slowly filled with ice-cold water, they froze solid before the water even reached the nozzles. Normally, boiler-fired warm water opened the hoses. I ran along the line trying to straighten the kinks, wildly hoping it would help. Before long came the sickening sound of the hoses ripping as the water inside expanded and burst the casings.

I turned, straightened my aching back, and watched the tinder-dry frame structures of Front Street go up in tall sheets of flame that crackled like lightning as the heat met the superchilled air. The collision of temperatures created an ice fog that settled ominously over the city as the fire raged out of control. Hundreds were racing this way and that, many with axes in hand. Abraham had disappeared.

I fell to helping the firemen who were trying to save Belinda Mulrooney's famous Fairview Hotel. Fast as we could, we soaked blankets in the puddles that were forming in front of the nearest burning building. Without a note of panic, the young Irishwoman called for hammers and nails and directed us to nail up the blankets to the front of her·hotel and the side facing the onrushing fire.

The inferno was about to reach the Pioneer Saloon just down the street. A man was surveying the shower of sparks between him and the front door and appeared to be on the verge of going inside.

"Gather up the money, McPhee," called Belinda Mulrooney. "The whole town's going to go!"

"Forget the money!" he shouted back, and ran inside. He appeared half a minute later staggering under an immense, antlered moosehead. "My good luck charm!"

It was chaos. The Dominion was up in flames, the Opera House, the Northern, Jamie's Palace Grand. .... Inside the tottering Bank of British North America, the vault burst open. Its heavy iron door was glowing red as the guts of a forge.

"What's to be done?" cried a man in front of the Aurora.

"Blow up the buildings in front of the fire!" commanded Captain Starnes of the Mounted Police. "Yours included!"

The Mountie dispatched a dog team to the Alaska Commercial Company warehouse for fifty pounds of blasting powder. I turned to work alongside thousands who'd showed up to help carry items of value from the buildings in harm's way out to the marsh behind the business district.

At one point I heard something yelled about Irish Nellie's boardinghouse, about it burning. I took off at full sprint.

The windows were all spouting flames when I got there; the back of the building was engulfed. Nellie and her terrified residents, many of whom were feeble or crippled, watched in disbelief from the street. When Nellie saw me she screamed, "Your brothers!"

"Where?" I yelled.

With a grimace, she pointed into the building. "Ethan—then Abe—brought everyone out. We heard Mrs. Jeffries's cries inside. Ethan went in after her, Abraham went after Ethan. Neither has come out!"

It might be only minutes, I knew, before the building collapsed. I scanned the onlookers gathered around and spotted one with an ax. I seized it and ran for the front door as Nellie screamed at me not to. A locomotive couldn't have dragged me away. On my hands and knees, I crawled in under the smoke billowing out the door. "Ethan!" I hollered at the top of my lungs. "Abraham!"

No reply, only groaning from upstairs.

Coughing, trying to hold my breath, I crawled up the stairs with the ax and bellied onto the oven-hot landing. I saw no one, nothing but smoke. At the end of a straight run, the hallway branched in two directions.

Suddenly Nuisance appeared from the hallway on the right. The dog recognized me and started barking, then disappeared where he'd come from. I followed to the fork in the hall and turned right, keeping low.

There they were, barely visible through the smoke. Ethan was pinned by a blackened timber, and so was a woman he'd shielded with his bulk. Abe was trying to pry the timber off Ethan with an ax.

"Jason, get out of here!" Abe ordered.

I kept bellying toward him.

This time he screamed, "You're going to get yourself killed!"

How could I turn and flee? I kept going.

Together, with both our axes, Abraham and I were able to pry the timber off and drag Ethan and the woman clear. "His leg's broke!" Abe yelled.

Ethan's face was a mask of pain. The woman had passed out.

Ethan started to rise on his good leg. "Stay down!" Abe ordered.

I dragged the woman on her back, by her collar, down the hallway; behind me came Abe, dragging Ethan.

The heat was overpowering and I couldn't breathe any longer. I thought I was about to black out. I grabbed up the woman, rose, and made my way down the stairs, the fury of the fire all around me.

In the street I laid the woman down and raced back inside. Halfway up the stairs I met them staggering down in the smoke. Leaning on Abe, Ethan was hopping down one step at a time, but neither one could breathe.

I took hold of Ethan on his other side. We lifted him and carried him into the street, where Nuisance, on three legs, was barking furiously.

A minute later the building was a skeletal tower of flame. It shortly tottered and collapsed. We were burned, but not too badly. The Hawthorn brothers were torn up, but we were alive.

SIX

The entire business district of Dawson City lay in ruins. One hundred seventeen buildings had been destroyed. On Front Street, Belinda Mulrooney's Fairview Hotel stood intact at the southern limit of the devastation, while the surviving landmark on the north end was the badly scorched Monte Carlo. The Palace Grand was nothing but cinders.

Miraculously, only one person died. In the ashes of the Bodega Saloon were discovered the badly charred remains of its co-owner, H. L. Watson, a known drinker. His demise went unmourned. The investigator for the Mounted Police named Watson as the lout who'd accidentally caused the disaster.

Only an hour before the blaze began, Watson was so drunk he had to be assisted upstairs to his apartment, one of several on the second floor. The bartender who'd undertaken this same assignment on a number of previous occasions dropped Watson, unconscious, in bed. As the bartender explained to the Mounties, he was able to manage inside Watson's room by the light of the lamp in the hallway, and he did not light the candle at Watson's bedside.

It was this candle, thoughtlessly mounted in a crude block of wood, that must have started the fire, the Mounties said. Watson had revived long enough to light the candle, then collapsed once more into his drunken stupor, never to wake again.

Before the ashes from the great fire had even cooled, the Golden City was rising once again like the phoenix. This time, the edifices of Front Street were going to be rebuilt on a grander scale. Some had been insured, like Donner's Bodega Saloon and Arizona Charlie's Palace Grand, but in many cases owners were left penniless. They had to sell their bare ground to rich men from the creeks eager to build commercial properties on prime Dawson real estate.

The boardwalk was going to be replaced by a concrete sidewalk, the street paved with macadam.

From the window of the hospital where Abe and I sat with Ethan, we could hear the orchestra of hammers and saws. We could see the freight wagons hauling the debris out and the fresh lumber in.

Ethan had a cast on his leg and was bandaged heavily on his back, arms, and face. Abe had burned both arms and scorched his eyebrows; I was burned some on my arms and the back of my left hand. The dog, in the corner, was worrying the bandage on his paw. "Stop that, Nuisance," I told him. Just as quickly I said to my brothers, "After what he did, I can't call him Nuisance anymore."

"Suppose not," Ethan said with grave cheerfulness.

"Sounds like if you picked the wrong hallway, you wouldn't have reached us in time. Give him a real name, Jason."

I thought about it. "It should have to do with staying with you two and burning his paw."

With three pairs of eyes on him, the dog yawned self-consciously. I was looking at his bandaged paw, the front right one. "What about Burnt Paw?"

"I like it," Ethan said. "Tells a story and sounds downright dignified."

Ethan proceeded to heave a huge sigh. "Brothers, I'll never touch another drink or place a nickel on green felt as long as I live."

"Amen to that," Abe said.

"Abraham . . . Jason . . . I have a confession to make."

"Out with it," Abe said. "After what we've been through, only suspense can kill us."

Ethan groaned like a man in hell. "I signed a document when I needed money. . . . I put up my third of the mill as collateral for a three-thousand-dollar personal loan from Cornelius Donner."

Abe went pale. "You couldn't have."

"I did. Now Abraham, what's done is done."

Abe reached for his hat. "I'm going to find our lawyer, the one who drew up our ownership document with Ladue. This can't be legal."

Ethan heaved another huge sigh. "I hope to God you're right."

With a glance over my shoulder at Ethan, I hurried after Abe, who was halfway out the door of the hospital. His limp was worse than usual, yet I could barely keep up with him on the way to the lawyer's office.

Our lawyer had already seen the document Ethan signed. Two lawyers Donner had sent earlier in the day had given him a copy of it. "In plain English, I'm afraid that *all three* of you are out," George Templeton told us. "Cornelius Donner has taken possession."

"Impossible!" Abe stormed.

I could scarcely breathe.

"It's all in the fine print down at the bottom there, I'm afraid. Donner secured the loan not merely with Ethan's third, but with yours and Jason's as well. Ethan may have been drunk when he signed it, and the value of what he signed away is far greater than the three thousand dollars he borrowed, but neither of those points constitute a defense, and it was properly witnessed. Remember when we first drew up the ownership papers, with Jason being absent, you wanted it stipulated that one could sign for all three."

Abe had to sit down. "I remember," he said. "But Ethan wasn't paying attention."

We left the law office in a state of shock and went directly to the mill. As we arrived, a new sign was being nailed up where the one with our name had stood. The new one read DONNER ENTERPRISES. The men gathered around us and wondered if we were really out of ownership. "Such appears to be the case," Abe admitted, still stunned.

The men said that they would have quit their jobs in sympathy if jobs weren't so hard to come by. They told us that their wages had been reduced from fifteen dollars a day to a hundred dollars a month.

"That's Dawson wages this spring," growled a burly man we didn't know.

"Who are you?" I demanded.

"The new foreman of this mill. You were paying too high."

Abe and I were allowed to gather our hand tools and

Ethan's, nothing more, not even a chair. Lock, stock, and barrel, the mill didn't belong to us anymore.

Donner appeared from inside the mill office with silver cane, Prince Albert coat, and every hair in place. Henry Brackett appeared at his elbow protectively, his eyes still a bit puffy from the beating Ethan had given him.

"I thought you were Ethan's friend," I said to Donner. "How could you do this to him?"

Donner ignored me. To Abraham he said with that phony, soothing baritone of his, "The little log cabin on the hill is still yours. I do hope you've put some savings by."

"We put everything back into the mill," Abe said flatly.

Donner touched the brim of his bowler with his gloved hand. "A pity. I congratulate you on your heroism of yesterday. You're the talk of the town—I'm sure you'll find employment."

Abe gave him a look that might have killed. For a moment it seemed Abe was thinking of the claw hammer in his hand as a weapon. Shoving the hammer instead through the loop in his nail apron, he said, "Let's go, Jason, before we give Dawson City something else to talk about."

I was burning up inside. As I turned on my heel, I made a vow to myself. We were going to get our mill back.

SEVEN

I worked the endless daylight hours of May as a carpenter, on Irish Nellie's new boardinghouse at first. One of the kings of the Klondike, Big Alex McDonald, had put up a generous amount for labor and materials to have her home for the downtrodden rebuilt as soon as possible.

If a man knew plumb and level and square, there was plenty of work in Dawson City. Not only was the entire business district under reconstruction, but so were the back streets, where frame houses for families were springing up in place of log cabins. Hundreds of women had traveled north the previous season to join husbands and sons. There was already a small legion of young children in town.

Abe and I were able to frame up one of these family houses every ten days. We seldom talked except about the work. Living in the shadow of our former life was a grim business. Dawson prices devoured our wages—a hundred dollars a month each.

Ethan wouldn't be able to join us until his leg mended. In the evenings, he tried to dispel the gloom inside the cabin. "We'll get back in the game, boys," he would say. "Our tide will come back in."

Despite the brave talk, I could hear it in Ethan's voice: His spirit was broken. He'd lost the mill for us, lost the dream of being our own bosses.

"I don't doubt it for a moment," Abe would agree stolidly, but in his eyes I could see the stamp of defeat.

Twenty years from now, I realized, my brothers could still be chafing under the bonds of what our father called "wage slavery."

For the time being I was keeping my vow concerning the mill to myself. I had a plan of sorts, and I was ready to take the next step.

I swallowed my pride and went to the mill to talk to Cornelius Donner. I was told to find him at his saloon, the New Bodega.

After being announced to Donner, I waited an hour amid the din of reconstruction before I was frisked and ushered up the stairs to the second floor of his saloon. In a plush chair in an unfinished room with a view onto Front Street, Donner was trimming his beard. With mirror in one hand, scissors in the other, and barely a glance in my direction, he said, "Close the door; I can't tolerate the sawdust."

Donner laid the scissors aside, lit a cigar, and began to draw on it. "Remember the *Maine*," he said sardonically. The smoothness of his voice grated on me.

"Cuban tobacco?" I guessed.

"The finest ... worth fighting for, I'd say.... Now, what brings the Hawthorn pup? Your brothers have sent you?"

Punctuating his thick sarcasm, Donner blew a cloud of smoke my way. I sat up straight, reminded myself why I was here. "I don't imagine that you care to run a sawmill," I said. "I came to find out what you'd sell it for."

The peacock was amused. After only a moment's reflection, he said, "Twenty thousand dollars."

We both knew he'd just pulled the figure out of the air. I said, "You must be forgetting that you have only 51 percent of the mill. The rest is owned by the heirs of Joseph Ladue, the founder of Dawson City, who set us up in business."

"Thank you so much for the history lesson. Yes, yes, Ladue's heirs will continue to be paid. Their lawyer here in Dawson has already seen to that."

"Even ten thousand for your 51 percent would be generous. Nobody else would pay you that much."

"Why are we having this discussion?" Donner snapped. His voice, suddenly harsh as a hacksaw blade, sounded nothing like the one he usually employed.

Next moment, he was back to his acid-smooth baritone. "Have you brought your pocketbook? Did you leave a suitcase full of nuggets downstairs?"

"I'll get the money. I just needed to know if you would sell."

"Now you know, but where will you get it? A rich aunt, perhaps?"

There was a smirk on his face, as if he were talking to a six-year-old.

I bristled. "I don't have an aunt—I'll get it in Nome."

Donner leaned back, blew a smoke ring, stroked his beard. "Ah," he said. "Nome." He began to chuckle softly.

"Don't laugh at me," I told him.

"I won't, then, until you're out of sight. Oh, by the way—I hear your brother Ethan broke his leg. Tell him I send my regards. It's a shame he'd never agree to another fight. Perhaps he'll reconsider once his leg mends, now that he is, shall we say, short on funds. . . . He's the Hawthorn I want to see."

"Maybe if he ever gets back in the ring it should be with you."

Donner laughed. "You're as insolent as that mongrel of yours! Now, if you'll excuse me, I'm off to the gym to sign a new fighter."

"Some rob with a gun, others with a fountain pen."

The scoundrel laughed again. "Pup, you can get away with speech like that only because we're in Canada. Don't push it—we might meet down the Yukon one day, in Alaska."

Still, I wouldn't leave. "Have you ever had calluses on your hands in your life, Donner?"

With a sly smile, he replied, "You assume I'm soft because I dress well. Appearances can be deceiving, as they say."

Donner leaned back in his chair, his hands behind his head, a contemptuous grin lighting his features. "Would you care to wrestle for my mill, right here, right now?"

"Of course I would. Is this a trick? What kind of wrestling?"

"No tricks—simple arm wrestling. On my desktop here."

"You swear you'll keep your word. . . ."

There was a devilish glint in his dark eyes. "Why would you doubt me?"

We knelt down on opposite sides of an end table and clasped hands. His grip was nothing less than powerful. But then, he outweighed me by thirty pounds, and he was in the prime of life.

"Whenever you say go," he said.

I thought I had a chance. Our forearms were the same length. I was strong. The trick was giving it my all immediately.

"Go!" I declared.

After only a moment's stalemate, Donner slammed my arm to the table with an overwhelming surge.

"Well," he said, standing up and straightening his vest. "Do come and see me if that aunt of yours leaves you her estate. As you anticipated, I might like to sell my mill."

I felt my face flushing red, more from humiliation than exertion. "If I'd beat you just now, you wouldn't have kept your word," I said on my way out.

"We'll never know, will we?" came his haughty reply.

After two weeks in the cabin, Ethan couldn't tolerate the confinement. He joined us as a sawyer. In a seated position, with the strength of his upper body, he could do almost all our sawing for us.

With Ethan came the dog. His bandage had come off, and Burnt Paw could run and leap and climb as well as ever. Yet standing at rest, he'd favor the right front paw as if it were freshly hurt. "Burnt Paw," I'd say, "there's nothing wrong with you. Put that paw down. Go on, put it down. You know what I'm talking about."

The mutt would cock his head, stand his ears up straight, look at me with that blue eye, and put the paw down on the ground. A minute later he'd be holding it up again. I wondered if he could remember the fire.

I wished I couldn't. I was still seeing flames wherever I turned, in glimpses at work when my mind would stray, and in my sleep. All night, it seemed, I was inside burning buildings with the timbers crashing down around me.

The middle of May brought ever-longer days, trickling water, and warnings not to walk on the Yukon—the ice was rotten. Out at the gold creeks, the mounds of muck brought up from the shafts bucket by bucket all winter had finally begun to thaw. It was possible for the miners to work aboveground at last, shoveling the pay dirt into sluice boxes running with diverted creekwater.

Cleanup at the creeks was bringing fabulous amounts of gold into town. "The doomsayers have been proven wrong," crowed the *Klondike Nugget*. "Dawson's wealth is no will-o'-the-wisp. Its citizens can be confident they are rebuilding on a foundation of solid gold."

Despite the newspaper's best efforts, all the talk on the streets was of Nome. Word came from over the Chilkoot that the Alaska Commercial Company and the North American Trading Company, both of which had big warehouses in Dawson City, already had new warehouses under construction in Nome. Suddenly all the naysayers, including Abe, knew that Nome was much more than the product of talk. Those two companies, headquartered in the States, were big business. A big discovery had indeed taken place at Nome, and the stampede was on.

The time was ripe to tell my brothers about my plans. "As soon as the ice breaks up," I told them, "I'm heading to Nome to stake a claim. I'll work it or I'll sell it. One way or the other, we're going to get the mill back."

They said nothing at first. A smile came to Ethan's face. I hadn't seen one there in a long, long time. "You always were our adventurer," he said. "Of course you'd give Nome a try."

"But this business about the mill," Abe added soberly, "shouldn't be a part of it. Go ahead, Jason, seek your own fortune. Don't chase a dream that can't come true. Ethan and I will find our way back into ownership somehow. It might not even be a sawmill. . . ."

"That mill fits us like a glove," I insisted. "I intend to have that sign restored one day: HAWTHORN BROTHERS SAWMILL. Donner will sell for ten thousand dollars, I think—he has no real interest in the mill. Keep in mind, Abe, claims on Bonanza Creek and Eldorado Creek sold for fifty thousand dollars before they were ever worked."

"Well, then," Ethan teased, "you'll have forty thousand left over. Don't you be surprised, Abraham, if Jason returns with the world tied up by its tail."

EIGHT

Dawson's milling crowds were anxious to leave town. At any time of day, a small throng could be found inspecting the maps of Alaska posted at the warehouses of the Alaska Commercial Company and the North American Trading Company. With Nome on my mind, I spent hours among them studying the course of the Yukon across the breadth of Alaska, and the shape of the coastline between the Yukon's delta and the new gold mecca, Nome.

I listened to the talk of hundreds of men. Aside from the word "gold," the next two mentioned most often were "breakup" and "steamboats." Breakup on the Yukon would bring the steamboats, and the steamboats would take them from Front Street fifteen hundred miles downriver to salt water, then fifty or sixty miles up the coast to the old Russian port of St. Michael.

Until the news of the new stampede, most of

Dawson's disappointed had planned to ship immediately south to the States from St. Michael. Now, with one last chance to strike it rich, most were planning to try Nome before they headed home. Transfer to an oceangoing steamer wasn't even necessary. A number of the Yukon River steamboats were going to proceed across the Norton Sound direct to Nome. In good weather, riverboats could make that crossing.

There were long lines for tickets, and it soon became apparent that the several dozen steamboats working the river wouldn't be able to accommodate everyone—not as soon as they wanted to go. For me, two hundred dollars for steamboat passage to Nome was out of the question. On top of that, the barest essentials for prospecting and wintering in Nome would cost well over a thousand dollars.

I had ninety dollars to my name, but I couldn't let that stump me. I'd left Seattle for the North with ten dollars in my pocket. If I could somehow make it to Nome and stake a claim, I would have something of value, something to work or to sell.

Some at Dawson who couldn't afford steamboat transportation were building scows or lashing together crude log rafts. In addition, there were hundreds of skiffs at Dawson—handsome rowed boats that had been made from whipsawed lumber at the Yukon's headwater lakes. Not that I could afford a skiff: Suddenly they were valuable. I considered joining with three or four others to buy one, but I'd heard enough about prospecting partnerships to know they usually ended in grief.

I'd rather go it alone. I'd paddle the remaining fifteen hundred miles of the Yukon in the same canoe I paddled the first five hundred, the green Peterborough I'd stowed a year ago behind our cabin. It was an eighteen-footer, identical to the one Jamie and her father had paddled to Dawson. "The finest made in Canada," Jamie had called it.

I'd head to St. Michael, then buy a thirty-dollar ticket for deck passage to Nome on one of the big steamers. The last leg across the Norton Sound would be a breeze.

By the time I got to Nome I'd be broke, but a claim stake wouldn't cost me a dime and neither would a rock to pound it in.

All my hopes were pinned on the condition of my canoe. I hadn't inspected it since I'd tipped it over a year before onto three short logs to keep it out of the dirt. The weight of snow could have broken its ribs; a porcupine could have chewed it up underneath.

As I headed home from the warehouse of the Alaska Commercial Company I was remembering what a splendid paddler Jamie was. It came with being a girl of the north country.

After nearly a year my memory of Jamie hadn't begun to fade. Those freckles on her nose were vivid as yesterday; so was her wavy black hair.

I slowed my stride and let my memory drift, and then I was back in Skagway, seeing her for the first time. I'd collapsed in the street and woken in a strange room to her voice and her hazel eyes.

I let my mind drift a little more and found myself perched on the bluff where Lake Lindeman spilled into the roily One Mile River. The scene came back clearly. There were Jamie and Homer down below, paddling their Peterborough expertly into the maw of the rapids.

By the time I was nearing the cabin, my memories had seated me in the Palace Grand, staring up at the stage at the confident wonder of her: Jamie, the Princess of Dawson.

I came back to the present and broke into a run. Behind the cabin, the fireweed was knee-high around the canoe and starting to bloom.

Carefully, I tipped the canoe over and eased it to the ground. My eyes ran up and down its frame. I could breathe easy. It was in perfect condition.

My paddle and my old spare were inside the cabin, cross mounted on the wall for decoration. It was time to put them back to use!

I sat in the grass by the canoe, enjoying the heat of the May sunshine. In addition to the fireweed, all sorts of other wildflowers were blooming around the cabin.

All winter, on account of Jamie, I'd been waiting for them. How many times in the last ten months had I recited that last stanza from her final performance? As she'd thrilled the house with the conclusion of her father's new poem, "My Heart Remains in the Northland," Jamie had kept her eyes on mine. Afterward, she'd confided that she'd written the stanza herself:

> *For though I roam in far-off climes,*
> *In my heart, dear friend, I'll be counting the time*
> *Till winter fades and breakup nears.*
> *So look for me when first flowers appear,*
> *I'll be on the first boat, and it will feel so grand,*
> *Because, don't you know—*
> *MY HEART REMAINS IN THE NORTHLAND!*

Now I lay back in the lush green grass, and I looked up at the first billowy clouds of summer sailing by overhead. I reached out for a wildflower—a bright blue lupine—plucked it, and put its stem between my teeth. A fragrance I decided must be Jamie herself wafted through my nostrils to my imagination, and I allowed myself to remember her in all her coltlike glory, intelligent and impulsive and direct as an arrow. I admitted to myself how much I'd counted on her fulfilling her promise, how devastated I'd been to learn that her father had died.

Arizona Charlie was right. Jamie would pursue a new life on the stage among her new acquaintances. It stood to reason that a girl of fifteen wouldn't travel alone to the ends of the earth because of a stanza she'd written for a poem, because of a boy she'd met on the stampede to the Klondike. She'd have a manager who'd have plans for her. They'd have offers from every theater she'd performed in across the country. Jamie's radiance was as genuine as a June day north of the Arctic Circle, and her effect on all those audiences would have been electric. By now she was undoubtedly performing as a dramatic actress on the stage, in what city I couldn't begin to guess.

No, I had no reason to hope that Jamie would return to Dawson City now that her world had turned upside down. I had no reason to hope that she was still "counting the time till winter fades and breakup nears." What were the chances that at this moment she was on her way back to fulfill her promise?

The honking of geese, the first of the season, brought me out of the gloom. I located the flock, a noisy V of forty or more, winging north down the river. The wild joy with which they were announcing their return stirred my heart and provoked my memory.

When it was just the two of us, Jamie had told me, "I'll be back for the summer season as surely as the swans and the geese."

"I'll be standing right here on the dock," I had promised.

Suddenly I realized that I had a problem. I was planning on pushing off for Nome as soon as it was safe to paddle. The first boat into Dawson from the Pacific couldn't possibly arrive until a week or ten days after that.

"I'll be on the first boat, and it will feel so grand—"

No, I couldn't follow the ice down the Yukon on the heels of breakup, at the head of the new stampede. I had to wait at least for that first boat. I wouldn't break a promise to Jamie for all the gold in Nome.

NINE

The prize money for the North American Trading Company's Second Annual Breakup Lottery was fourteen thousand dollars and growing. I bought six chances at a dollar apiece—not that I mentioned this first fling at gambling to Abe. If I won he wouldn't fault me. I would quickly arrange the purchase of the sawmill, then launch my canoe and point it downriver: Nome was a magic word, and I wasn't going to miss the pure adventure of it. I'd be back on my own hook.

Everybody knew that breakup happens in the last two weeks of May or the first couple days of June. The person who guessed closest to the day, the hour, and the minute of the beginning of breakup would collect the prize money. On a hunch, I guessed it would be a few days later than the previous year; I put all my eggs into May 29's basket. For the exact time, I devised a system. Burnt Paw was my audience as I was thinking it up. We were outside the North American warehouse, on their dock, where I had a good view of the river ice.

"Listen carefully, Burnt Paw. For the hour, I'm going to put all six tries on six A.M." His ears stood up high and his bent tail beat a rhythm on the planking.

"You know why? The six stands for June, the month that the steamboats from the Pacific first arrive. Now for the minutes. I'll spread out my six chances. For starters, I'll pick three for the number of legs you like to stand on. You look dubious, my friend."

I rubbed Burnt Paw behind the ears the way he liked, and scratched his belly. Burnt Paw spent as much time with me these days as with Ethan, maybe because I talked to him so much.

"I'll pick seventeen because I turned seventeen last month; twenty-three for Ethan's current age; thirty for the number of days in the month Jamie was born, which is April; forty-five for the number of states in the Union; and fifty-six for the minimum number of years I'd like to spend in the North with Jamie."

Breakup indeed came on the twenty-ninth day of May. We were on our way to work, taking it slow on the hill below the cabin—Ethan was still on his crutches. That first crack from the river ice came loud as the shearing gates of eternity.

"Breakup!" I exclaimed. "Abe, quick—what time is it?"

Abe was the keeper of the gold watch that had been our father's. That old piece was as dependable as a ship captain's.

Disapproval written large across his face, Abe slowly pulled it out of his pocket by its chain, then hesitated. "Open it!" I said. "There's no black widow spider in there!"

By now half of Dawson had poured onto Front Street. Finally Abe opened the watch.

"Thirty-three minutes after six!" I declared. I knew I had a ticket that was awfully close.

Abraham glared at Ethan. "You didn't gamble on that breakup lottery?"

With his hearty laugh, Ethan declared, "For God's sake, no."

I took off running toward the North American warehouse.

"Did you, Jason?" Abe called after me.

I noticed the mutt's ears flapping at my side. "No," I called back, "but I couldn't stop Burnt Paw!"

By the time I reached the river, thousands were crowding the embankment watching the Yukon's yearly reminder of how puny all our efforts were compared to Nature's.

Burnt Paw barked at the colliding shards of ice as if they were animate beings. Many of them were house sized, and all were in motion. Their movements were chaotic but generally downstream. The hissing and grinding and cracking made a deafening din.

Accompanied by Burnt Paw, I made my way to the warehouse office to learn my fate. I had a very strong feeling that the mill would be ours again by nightfall.

A throng had gathered. By the office window of the warehouse, a sign had been posted with the heading EXACT TIME OF BREAKUP—DAY, HOUR, MINUTE. As I arrived, a clerk with a thin mustache and a grave expression had written a large 29 under DAY, and now he wrote 6 A.M. under HOUR. Shouts went up from a dozen or so throats, one of them mine.

Now for the telling minute . . . All my hopes were on my ticket for May 29, 6 A.M. and 30 minutes.

The clerk paused tantalizingly with his marker in midair.

"Out with it, you donkey!" someone yelled.

Under MINUTES, with a quick flourish, the clerk jotted down 32.

I felt as if I'd been hit with destiny's golden bolt. I was only two minutes off. Surely I'd won!

As I reached in my pocket for my tickets, a woman shrieked from the back, "It might be me!"

The crowd parted, revealing a woman gray before her years who was picking up her skirts and starting forward.

The lady was telling people at her elbow what her number was, but I couldn't hear for all the commotion. Seconds later her number passed through the throng like wildfire and left me jubilant as a fish on a drying rack. Hers—31—was one minute closer than mine. One minute!

A minute later the clerk verified that no one had bought a ticket for thirty-two minutes after the hour. "We have a winner!" he declared.

Word was passed, to much approval, that the woman worked at a dressmaking and millinery shop. A check for $17,463 was waiting for her at the bank! At least a rich man wasn't going to pocket the prize, I consoled myself.

Suddenly I saw a flash of silver from the corner of my eye. In the same instant came a yelp from Burnt Paw. He'd been struck!

"Donner!" I yelled, recognizing the rogue in fancy clothes behind the silver cane. "Why did you do that?"

I lifted Burnt Paw up so that he wouldn't be trampled by Donner or anyone else.

"Because the cur was in my way, everybody's way."

Burnt Paw, whose face was now nearly level with the eyes of his tormenter, began to growl.

Donner lifted his cane menacingly; Burnt Paw growled even louder.

I held tight, not knowing what Burnt Paw might do. "You knew he was ours."

"I didn't. I didn't even see you until after I'd struck him. But now that you mention it, I have seen the mongrel before. I have a keen memory. . . . When was it . . . ? Yes, on the street, the day your brother defended the dog's right to the boardwalk."

Burnt Paw was still growling. "It seems like he has a keen memory, too," I said. "Something tells me you should make an effort to stay out of his way."

Donner burst out laughing. "You're no wrestler, Hawthorn, but you're a fine comedian."

Within two days the river was spotted by only occasional floes. To the cheers of hundreds and cries of "Nome or bust!" and "Hurrah for Nome!" dozens of parties started downriver on scows and log rafts, smart-looking skiffs too. The *W. K. Merwyn*, a creaky little steamboat that had dry-docked in Dawson for the winter, set off with standing room only.

I was in a high panic that these rushers and thousands more would stake all the beaches at Nome that had gold in them before I could get there. All the same I stood fast as a pillar of salt, struck immobile by the possibility, however remote, of Jamie's return.

Abe said, "You're waiting another day or two for the river to be completely ice-free, eh, Jason?"

"It's a fragile craft, your canoe," Ethan chimed in.

I had to tell them I was waiting for Jamie, for the possibility she would return. So that's what I did. I told them about the conversation we'd had when she'd left Dawson back in July.

They already knew about her father's death. I wasn't surprised that Abe looked doubtful. "Maybe you should get going while there's time."

Ethan, still a dreamer at heart, said, "You're doing the right thing, Jason. If you want, I'll greet the rest if she isn't on the first one. That way, I can tell her how you were there to meet the first one and are dying to see her when you return from Nome—a conquering hero."

"Now you both know," I said. "I'm a fool for love."

"I'm sure there's no greater cause," Abe allowed.

While I was waiting I started to assemble an outfit for my journey downriver. In pawnshops I rummaged among the castoffs from the tens of thousands of stampeders who'd passed through Dawson. My eyes took in rifles and shotguns selling for only a dollar or two apiece; clothing from gum boots to prospectors' hats; rope, canvas, goldpans, picks, shovels, and mosquito netting; even medicines like Dr. Kilmer's Swamp Root, Kidney, Liver and Bladder Cure. I bought rope and canvas and mosquito netting, and oilskin sacks for dry storage of flour, sugar, beans, and evaporated foods such as dried fruit and soup vegetables. A bald vendor with a sense of humor threw in Dr. Kilmer's Cure for free.

More and more boats were setting off downriver. Watching them go made me sick in the pit of my stomach. After a while I stopped watching. Simply hearing the gunshots as they launched and all the shouts of "Nome or bust!" had the same effect. I was losing my chance at Nome's golden beaches.

Within days, the Yukon was threatening to flood Dawson as it had the year before. The entire town, including the three of us—Ethan's cast was freshly removed—

stood shoulder to shoulder sandbagging the top of the riverbank. As we labored, hundreds of boatloads of new Klondike hopefuls pulled in from the lakes at the head of the Yukon—Tagish and Bennett and Lindeman. It was a puny fleet compared to the navy of '98.

The river crested as it lapped at the sandbags. Dawson was spared flood on the heels of fire.

Most of Dawson's new arrivals stayed no longer than to gawk at the sights and to buy supplies. Most of these gaunt men and women had overwintered in canvas tents along the shores of Bennett and Lindeman five hundred miles upstream. By now they'd heard the news that the rest of us had learned a year before. The rich ground had been staked by prospectors already along the Yukon when gold was discovered clear back in August of '96.

In great numbers, the newcomers put Dawson at their backs and rushed downriver. To my dismay almost all of them had their sights freshly set on Nome.

Eight in the evening on June 12, the Hawthorn brothers were eating supper at our little table outside the cabin. The sun was still high. As ever, I was keeping watch on the farewell bend a couple miles below Dawson, where the Yukon turned a corner and disappeared under a big landslide scar that looked like a scraped mooseskin.

One moment it wasn't there and the next it was: a big, bright sternwheeler, plowing its way around the bend and spouting a cloud of white smoke from its stack. I blinked a few times, thinking I was imagining it, until I heard the chuffing of its exhaust. Half a second later came a mighty whistle blast and then two more. Burnt Paw got up from under the table, perked up his ears, and stood facing town and the river. "First boat," Ethan said.

"Big, fancy one—bet it's the *Yukoner*. Fastest boat on the river last season."

Within seconds, thousands of people streamed out of Dawson's buildings and onto the streets. I steeled myself against disappointment as I rose and said calmly, "I think I'll run down there and join the first-boat celebration."

Ethan winked and said, "You run along, Jason. I'm off my feet for the day."

"Think I'll stay with Ethan," Abe said. "You go with Burnt Paw. Good luck, Jason. You never know—she might be on that boat."

I grabbed my broad-brimmed prospector's hat, the one I'd worn coming over the Chilkoot, for good luck.

I walked a bit, then broke into a run. My heart was in my throat. All the while came the booming blasts of the steam whistle. I couldn't see the sternwheeler anymore for the buildings as I ran through the back streets. "Faster, Burnt Paw!" I yelled, and the mutt ran in front of me, looking back, ears flapping. At one point he got tangled up underfoot and I almost went down.

A brass band was playing a march as I reached Front Street. On the river side of the street and spilling down the Yukon's bank, thousands jostled for a good view. Burnt Paw lent his shrill voice to the canine cacophony. People were shouting, children running back and forth. . . .

Burnt Paw and I squirmed our way across Front Street to the embankment.

Now I could see the lettering—it was the *Yukoner*—and passengers on all three decks crowding the rails, waving their hats. I could see plenty of dresses, but I couldn't see faces.

The fancy white sternwheeler nosed into the dock

and the boat was tied up. At last I could see faces. Passengers began to come down the gangplank. I studied every woman's face, suddenly doubting I'd be able to recognize Jamie's.

It took only a matter of minutes for the *Yukoner* to empty out. I fell in a heap to the ground, realizing the damage my hopes had done me.

Then there was one more passenger, under a straw hat in a bright summer dress. A young woman? A girl? I stood up, watching closely as she struggled with a large leather suitcase.

The young woman looked at the crowd up and down the bank, her eyes searching, darting this way and that.

Her hair was black as a raven's wing.

Our eyes met.

"Jamie!" I cried.

"Jason!" she called. "Jason!"

TEN

Jamie stepped off the gangplank and we embraced. I kissed her on the cheek, two, three times as she heaved a sob and I recognized, close-up, those few precious freckles on her nose. We held each other. Jamie was trembling and so was I. When she broke away, tears were streaking her eyes. In one hand was a roll of parchment; her free hand searched a dress pocket. "Oh, where's my handkerchief? My kingdom for a handkerchief!"

Not finding one, Jamie wiped her eyes with the back of her hand, and then she reached out and dabbed my tears from my cheekbones. "I told myself a hundred times coming up the river that I wouldn't fall apart," she began. "Look what I've done. It's not like me."

I wasn't even sure I could speak.

"I knew you'd be here, Jason. Right here waiting for me, like you said you would. Who's this? It looks like you've found a friend."

For a moment I was confused, then I followed her eyes to the bent tail rapping the ground. "That's Burnt Paw," I replied.

"I can see he's favoring that front right paw. You little ragamuffin," Jamie cooed as she swept him up in her arms. Burnt Paw rolled his eyes. His quick tongue caught her chin.

"I love your half-and-half face. And those ears, where'd you get them? Off a flying fox from Borneo? This paw, did you burn it? Is that how you got your name?"

I reached for her suitcase. "In the Dawson fire," I said. "Late April."

Jamie set Burnt Paw down. "I heard about the fire. . . ."

"How? How did the news ever reach a telegraph?"

"By dogsled to Skagway, by boat to Seattle. What a sight coming around the bend to see Dawson already rebuilt!"

With these words Jamie took three bounding leaps to the top of the embankment, no matter that she was wearing a dress. "Come up, Jason. Look, here's a bench over the Yukon. The Golden City is even more splendid than I remembered!"

I sat down beside her, took her hand. "Jamie, I can't believe I'm not dreaming."

Her voice was etched with sadness as she replied, "'We are such stuff as dreams are made on, and our little life is rounded with a sleep.' I came across that in one of Shakespeare's plays, and I've discovered it's true."

"I'm so sorry you lost Homer. Arizona Charlie told me this spring."

Her father's name spoken out loud brought fresh

tears to her luminous hazel eyes. "It was so sudden, Jason. I had no chance to ask his blessing or what I should do without him. We never had a chance to say good-bye."

"I'm glad I knew him, Jamie. I never told you this, but I used to imagine birds nesting in his beard."

"I love that. What kind of birds?"

"Bluebirds. No, Canada geese."

"Yes, it was that enormous." I'd made her laugh.

"He was a great poet," I added, "but an even better man."

"Thank you." Jamie sniffled, finding her handkerchief at last in another dress pocket. "Father always said he was a simple cobbler of verses, not a real poet. He'd say, 'Leave immortality to the Bard of Avon, Bobby Burns, Lord Tennyson, and such. I'll always be able to skin a moose and paddle a canoe better than I can write a line of poetry.' People loved him, Jason. He was kind."

She took her hand from mine and petted Burnt Paw behind his head.

"You look older," I began again. "Grown-up. And more beautiful than ever."

"I just turned sixteen."

"On the last day of April."

"More recently, on the last day of May."

I was jolted. "How many days are there in May?"

"Thirty-one, last time I checked."

"I would have tied, if only I'd remembered your birthday!"

"Whatever do you mean, Jason?"

"There was a lottery on the beginning of breakup."

"I remember last year's."

"Well, I had a system of sorts. If only I'd remembered

your birthday, I would have split the prize with a seamstress. I'd have nearly nine thousand dollars!"

Understandably, Jamie was still confused. "That's a shame, Jason. . . . I suppose my birthday will be unforgettable now, eh?"

"That's for sure, but enough of that! Breakup is spilt milk, water under the bridge, and there are no bridges over the Yukon."

"I could listen to you mix metaphors all day."

"How long was your journey?"

"Fourteen days up the Yukon from St. Michael, after an ocean voyage of three weeks, on the *Ohio*. We sailed the fourth of May."

"Where did you sail from?"

"Seattle—I was thinking of you."

"Were the seas rough?"

"Don't I still look green? Imagine a steamer with seven hundred souls aboard tossed around like a toy! We were caught by a spring storm in the Gulf of Alaska and thrown off course. It's a wonder we didn't end up in Japan."

"Seven hundred people? Where were they going—not to Dawson City?"

"To Nome! Stampeding to Nome!"

"Stop, I'm ill. Seven hundred to Nome—I was hoping to stake a claim on the beach."

"It had better be a long beach. A tent city has sprung up—I saw a photograph—and prospectors are at work with sluice boxes and rockers along the beach and all the nearby creeks. I was tempted just to go see it. It's like the Klondike all over again, only no need to cross mountains and build boats and float a river."

"They don't talk about Dawson City anymore?"

"Except to say it's no place to get rich. This time last

year, people wore buttons that said YES, I'M GOING. This
year, the word 'Klondike' is synonymous with folly. To
brush someone off, instead of saying something like, 'Go
peddle your papers,' people say, 'Aw, go to the Klondike.'"

"But *you* came. . . ."

I meant to say it full of feeling, but it came out like a
dying duck in a thunderstorm. I wanted those three
words to say that I loved her. I was half certain that in
response she would profess that she'd come these thousands of miles solely for my sake.

I thought she might take my hand, but she didn't.
Jamie glanced at me, avoiding a full meeting of the eyes,
and her gaze went out onto the river, where the swells
of the Yukon rolled swiftly downstream. "My heart remains in the Northland," she said with an enigmatic
smile, and stood up briskly.

I was left with the awful uncertainty of wondering if
it was the North she'd returned for, or for me. If it was
both, what percentage of her heart did I have a claim to?

At a loss, I asked, "What's that parchment in your
hand?"

"Oh, this! It was posted on the boat. By now they
must be plastered all over Dawson City."

It was a poster that she unrolled. Its headline proclaimed THE GREAT RACE.

"What is it, Jamie?"

"A race from Dawson City to Nome. It's the Alaska
Commercial Company's answer to the N.A.T.'s breakup
lottery. Isn't it exciting? Here, I'll read it to you. I know it
almost from memory:

> *"The Alaska Commercial Company announces*
> *the Great Race from the riverbank at Dawson*
> *City, Canada, to its warehouse in Nome, Alaska.*

*Attention, all those who would compete in the
greatest marathon the world has ever seen, from
the established gold capital of the North to its new
twin on the Bering Sea.*

"*If you would brave all comers and conditions
for the prize of $20,000, register with the Alaska
Commercial Company in Dawson City anytime
up to the firing of the starting gun at noon three
days after the first steamboat bearing this news
reaches our representatives at the mouth of the
Klondike River, namely Dawson City.*

"*To enter, contestants must contribute a $50
nonrefundable entry fee to the prize. Any shortfall
between fees collected and the $20,000 prize is to be
paid for by the sponsor, the Alaska Commercial
Company.*

"*Rules are as follows:*

"*1) Two-man teams only. If more than the two
who are registered for the race are in the craft, they
may not assist locomotion of the craft.*

"*2) The same pair that begins the race must
finish, with no substitutions en route.*

"*3) Contestants may travel by water, land,
or air.*"

"Land!" I interrupted. "There are no roads between
here and Nome. I doubt there are even trails. And what
could they mean, 'by air'?"

Jamie laughed. "By balloon? The fellow who wrote
this was so full of hot air, he could have inflated a fleet of
them. Here, I'll finish it up:

"*4) Teams need not finish with the same craft
they started with, but at no time is any form of*

assist from motor craft, such as a steamboat, permissible.

"5) An official of the A.C.C. from Dawson, bearing the list of entrants, will travel to Nome to serve as the judge at the finish line. The decision of the judge is final.

"Hear ye, hear ye, join the Great Race across Alaska and thence to Nome!"

Jamie rolled up the parchment. "The trip down the river is a journey of epic proportions. Of course, there's still the Norton Sound to deal with after that."

"What a race!"

We looked into each other's eyes, asking the same question.

Jamie said it first. "What do you think, Jason? Did I hear you say you were headed to Nome anyway?"

"I still have my Peterborough," I replied. "I've paddled the first five hundred miles of this river, but that's the sum total of my experience. I once knew a girl who was an artist with a canoe paddle. . . ."

Jamie was beaming. "We'd be lunatics!" With that, she stifled a sudden yawn. "I'm exhausted. Let's see how we feel tomorrow, Jason. I should think about where I'm going to stay."

"Belinda Mulrooney's Fairview?" I suggested, pointing. "Where you lived with your father?"

She looked long at the hotel. I saw anxiety creasing her forehead.

"I should have realized, Jamie. The Fairview would only make you sad."

"It's not that. . . . My first night back in Canada, I'd prefer to sleep outdoors, if that's possible."

I was delighted, and I already had an idea. "How

about our storage tent in the yard outside the cabin? It's under a big spruce, which will help to darken it enough for you to sleep. We can move out a few things. We've got a cot and a sleeping bag for you."

"That will do it. I'll sleep like a stone, midnight sun or no."

Jamie looked all around, at the river and the town and the landslide scar like a moosehide on the mountain that towered above Dawson. "I'm home. Lead on, Jason."

ELEVEN

Jamie slept through the arrival of four sternwheelers the following morning. My brothers had gone to work, and Burnt Paw and I were watching the swarming activity all along the Yukon's bank. The steamboats from the Pacific added color and size to the flotilla of hundreds of boats assembling for the assault on Nome.

My eyes kept darting over to the tent where Jamie was sleeping, not twenty yards away. My mind was racing with unanswered questions, the first being, Would Jamie really join me in the race to Nome? The two of us, down the Yukon? The prospect was too exciting to be believed.

If we did try it, what were our chances with the canoe?

Suddenly Jamie appeared in the grass next to me.

"Your dress . . . ," I said.

"I slept in it. Would you look at what's going on along

the river! Boats from up at the mouth of the Klondike to clear past town."

"It's like the word 'Nome' is written large across the sky."

"We have to decide about the race, don't we? But first, I'm starving! There's only one meal I've been craving all this time."

"What would that be?"

"Flapjacks and bacon."

"In that case, I can take care of you right here at Jason's Café."

As soon as we'd eaten, Jamie wanted to inspect the canoe. We tipped it upright, and she pronounced it in perfect condition. Seating herself in the stern, Jamie closed her eyes and began to stroke with an imaginary paddle.

When she opened her eyes, she said, "Your Peterborough is like an old friend."

We walked around the side of the cabin for another look at the crowded banks of the Yukon. Jamie shaded her eyes and gave the fleet a long, careful appraisal. "They're all scows or rowed boats," she said finally. "I don't see any canoes. But then, that shouldn't be surprising. I wonder what became of mine and Father's after he sold it."

"I can't remember the last time I saw a canoe. They always were a rarity."

"When it comes to the race," Jamie said, "no one could match your canoe in a sprint, but fifteen hundred miles down the Yukon is no sprint. I woke up thinking that if we go to shore to sleep, and surely we'll need to sleep . . ."

"That whole navy will pass us by. I've been thinking the same thing."

"On a scow," Jamie said tentatively, "we could set up a tent for sleeping. For cooking, we could make a mud hearth or even set up a Yukon stove. There's no doubt we could float twenty-four hours a day, but of course a scow is nothing but a floating platform and we couldn't go any faster than the current."

Jamie fell to scratching Burnt Paw behind his ear while her eyes drifted down the river in a thoughtful trance.

I was pondering, too. A nice, sleek skiff was what we really needed. The only problem was, rowed boats of any description had become more and more valuable with half of Dawson, it seemed, rushing to Nome. Even before the race was announced, skiffs were selling for hundreds of dollars.

A skiff today might cost five hundred or more. It seemed lunacy to suggest spending such an amount on a simple wooden boat, but our chances might depend on it.

"What about a skiff?" I suggested, thinking Jamie had arrived with a large sum of money.

Jamie brightened. "We'd pass the scows by like they were fastened to the bottom! We could carry a world of gear and grub, with room to stretch out and sleep. Not only that, a sturdy skiff might be able to handle the Norton Sound between St. Michael and Nome. There must be a hundred and fifty of them down there. Maybe someone would sell."

Our eyes were asking each other the identical question, but Jamie spoke first. "Can you afford a rowed boat, Jason?"

"No," I answered, and I realized that this was the time to tell her of the calamity that had befallen me and my brothers. I told it all, from the moment that the

Sydney Mauler was about to boot Burnt Paw into the street that day in March, to Ethan's rise and fall, to the fire and the loss of the mill. In distress, Jamie listened intently. At last I said, "All this to explain that I can't afford a rowboat. After the supplies I've bought in the last week, I have twenty dollars to my name. Jamie, I'm back in poverty's basement."

She heaved a sigh. "We've landed there together then—add my wealth to yours and we have sixty dollars."

It was my turn to be surprised and dismayed. "There's no money to be made on the stage?"

"That's not it—I was one of the lucky few. We were making so much money it seemed like water out of a faucet, but Father kept spending like there was no tomorrow. After his life in the bush, mostly trading for whatever he needed, spending was a novelty he couldn't resist. When he died I had little more than enough to get back to the North. It cost fifteen hundred dollars to get here from Philadelphia!"

I told her of my vow to buy the mill back from Cornelius Donner, that I'd thought I could accomplish it by staking a claim in Nome.

"You might get there in time to stake a worthwhile claim—it depends on the extent of those golden beaches. But there must be several thousand people already there, with more on the way."

"I know—I'm ill thinking about it."

"I'd almost prefer our chances of winning the race, even if we can't afford a skiff. Your canoe—as far as it would take us—will be our good luck charm."

"I always fancied you were born with a paddle in your hands."

"Funny you said that—Father always said so. He

would like our chances as far as the river will take us. I believe we could arrange the gear in such a way that one of us could sleep on it while the other paddled. We could be hundreds of miles ahead when we reach the sea."

"At the mouth of the Yukon, we trade for an ocean-going craft?"

With a nod, Jamie said, "I can't picture if the racers will attempt to cross the sound or will be forced to hug the coastline all the way to Nome. The latter, I would think. The only thing we know for sure is that there's much more that we don't know than what we do know."

I laughed. "That's what will make it an adventure. We'll cross that bridge when we come to it—if only there were a bridge."

Jamie chuckled at my nonsense.

"What will you do with your half of the prize money?" I asked.

She laughed. "Aren't you counting your chickens a little early?"

"I'm just being optimistic. What do you say, then?"

Her eyes were lit with competitive fire. "If we're going to Nome anyway, to try our chances on those golden beaches, why not join the race? If we fail, and then we go bust prospecting, we'll work our way back to Dawson by winter, chopping boiler wood for the riverboats if necessary. We can't be much broker than we are now."

"We're partners, then!"

"Partners!"

"Good. Splendid. I was afraid . . ."

"Afraid of what, Jason?"

"I was afraid that with it being just the two of us, you wouldn't."

Her hazel eyes, dead serious, met mine. "I trust you, Jason. You're a gentleman. I know you."

"Thank you," I replied. "Yes, you'll always be able to trust me."

"Let's hurry, then! We have so much to do and so little time. My clothes will be useless on the river. I need to find trousers and shirts and such. Gum boots . . . a wide-brimmed prospector's hat like yours."

"Men's clothes, like you wore coming over the Chilkoot."

"Yes, or the country will eat me alive—especially the mosquitoes. I don't suppose that any woman on the trail was less a woman for wearing practical clothes."

"I hope your hair isn't an inconvenience."

"You like it long? It's much longer than when you saw me last."

"I love it past your shoulders like that. It would be a great tragedy if you had to cut it."

I realized I was blushing.

Jamie giggled and gave me a poke. "Then I won't."

On the morning of June 15, race day, the riverbank was bedlam. With several hours left until the noon starting gun, 329 teams of two had already registered for the Great Race. Add to those 329 boats the eleven steamboats now docked in Dawson and the various and sundry craft not participating in the race, and it was only by luck that we found a sliver of water to float our canoe. With all the shouting and the comings and goings on all sides as the boats were being loaded, it was a scene of the utmost confusion.

Abe and Ethan helped us load. They were nearly as excited as we. I should have known I could count on my brothers. They'd given us our fifty-dollar entry fee, which allowed us to complete our outfit with our funds. At the last, Jamie spent six dollars on a shotgun of the

same make as her father's, shells to go with it, and a
canoe paddle for a spare. Five dollars was all we had left
to spend downriver.

It was ten minutes before noon when Jamie stowed
the shotgun under the lashing that crisscrossed the oilskin tarp covering our gear. "All set," she said, giving her
wide-brimmed hat a good tug on her forehead. She'd
braided her hair into a lively black rope that swung back
and forth as she worked.

Abe and Ethan were watching, their eyes twinkling.
The men on either side were equally entranced—we
were wedged between two skiffs, each of which had
two rowing stations. "What do you aim to do with that
shotgun, miss?" a grizzled fellow asked her. "Blast your
competitors?"

"If we run out of grub," Jamie told him good-
naturedly.

"Cannibals in the race, Harry. What is the world
coming to?"

"How do you aim to cross the Norton Sound in that
wee bucket?" called an Irishman from the skiff on the
opposite side.

"We've got a balloon in our outfit," I volunteered.
"We aim to inflate it, tie on with the canoe, and fly to
Nome. It's legal, I hear. You watch for us—we'll wave."

There was laughter all around.

Jamie and I shook hands with my brothers. They
wished us Godspeed. Burnt Paw seemed to know exactly what was going on, and was leaping around us
like a jack-in-the-box. Anticipating the starting gun,
I snatched up my paddle and made ready to board.
Suddenly Burnt Paw launched himself into the canoe.

"I'd say he wants to go with you," Ethan observed.

The men on either side were now seated in their

rowing stations and poised for the gun. They barely cracked a grin at our foolishness.

I grabbed Burnt Paw and set him down on the bank. He immediately lifted the one paw up, with the wrist slack. "You be a good boy," I said.

He whined and he whimpered.

"Take him with you for good luck," Ethan insisted. "You never know when he might come in handy."

"One minute!" a voice from upriver boomed.

I boarded and, keeping low, made for the bow. Standing in six inches of water in her gum boots, Jamie pushed off enough to float the canoe free. She stepped carefully into the stern; then we paddled a few strokes until we were abreast of the bows of the neighboring skiffs.

Jamie took a look around. She gave me a smile more golden than the midnight sun. "Take a deep breath, Jason."

I heard Burnt Paw's shrill bark. I heard my brothers calling "Good luck!" and "Ho for Nome!" The starting gun went off, loud as a cannon.

Amid the shouts and the cheers and the splashing of oars, it was pandemonium.

"Watch our smoke!" I yelled. "Nome or bust!"

Jamie and I started paddling in earnest, and our canoe shot forward. With a glance over my shoulder toward my brothers, as I freed a hand to give them a last wave, I saw Burnt Paw in the river. Waterworthy as any muskrat, he was paddling after us with all his might.

I stopped paddling, I was laughing so hard. "Jamie!" I cried. "Look behind us!"

Here came that mongrel, with only his black-and-white face above water, his ears hinged forward with determination. The shore was slipping away; my brothers were bent over laughing. We were about to be swept into the boils at the edge of the main current.

Jamie spun the canoe sideways so that Burnt Paw would have a wider target. I stowed my paddle and made the catch. "Down the Yukon!" Jamie shouted. "Three for Nome!"

TWELVE

Burnt Paw shook himself out, ran atop the gear to Jamie, then back to me in an instant, his bent tail wagging faster than I'd ever seen it. I lifted him high so my brothers could see he hadn't drowned, then set him down and retrieved my paddle as they gave us a last wave.

The lower end of Front Street was sliding by, and shortly we were under the landslide scar downstream of Dawson.

A few minutes later, almost at the rear of the fleet, we entered the farewell bend. We stopped paddling and looked upstream over our shoulders. "There it goes," Jamie said, and we watched the Golden City disappear as if, after all, it were only an illusion. There went its hotels and dance halls, its warehouses, all the houses and cabins dotting the hills.

Suddenly there was only the wilderness, the bush, with no hint of civilization along the Yukon's shores.

Yet on all sides we were hemmed in by boats. "Let's see if we can put some of them behind us!" Jamie called from the stern, and I replied joyously, "It will be my pleasure!"

Stroke after stroke, I paddled hard, not so fast that I'd run short of breath or throw Jamie off behind me, but with all the controlled power I could muster.

At the back of the canoe, Jamie was steering as well as paddling. She had an uncanny sense for where the current ran swiftest, and always kept us in the fastest water. With the last fraction of every stroke, she adjusted the canoe's direction while staying in tandem with my paddle.

We were flying. We were overtaking the scows that were nothing more than clumsy platforms of milled lumber, the crude log rafts that wallowed in the troughs between the swells, even the skiffs with two men rowing. Some of the oarsmen nearly burst their lungs trying to match us before they lay up, panting.

Standing at the big sweep oars of the scows or straining at the oars of rowed boats, nearly everyone we passed put in their two cents' worth: "What's the hurry? You off to a fire?" "Did somebody tell you there's a race going on?" "Criminy, we're being passed by a girl." "Haven't you heard—Nome is upstream." "I think I've seen that girl somewhere before." "Is that yapper a dog or a water rat?" "Watch your talk, Clarence, that animal's got a shotgun and he no doubt shoots straighter than you."

"Don't worry, they'll have to take that canoe ashore in order to sleep," we heard more than a few times, but we were fairly certain our competition was underestimating our capacity for discomfort.

All the while Burnt Paw ran back and forth on the

gear, barking shrilly. We advised him to desist, but he had a mind of his own. Amid the confusion we just kept paddling, giving friendly waves when the faces were friendly. They almost always were.

The Yukon in this first stretch was running narrow and swift at the bottom of a fjordlike defile. Six miles from Dawson, according to my map, here came Fort Reliance, an abandoned trading post. We quit paddling as we watched it glide by on the right. We drank from our water flasks. The wind had come up, and with all the lint blowing from the cottonwoods lining the river, we were in the midst of a sort of snowstorm. We could barely make out the leaders downriver; there weren't very many of them. "We got here awful fast," I observed.

Jamie pulled from her pocket the gold watch that had been her father's and opened it up. "Forty-five, maybe fifty minutes," she reported.

"So we're going about eight miles an hour, right? Let's figure out how many days it will take us to reach the mouth of the river."

"That would be . . . around eight days," Jamie said, squinting her eyes as she calculated. "If we paddled at this rate every hour of every day." Then she broke out laughing.

"I guess you're right. We can't expect to be logging eight miles an hour all the way down the Yukon. But it gives us something to aim for."

"Look, another Peterborough!" Jamie exclaimed. She pointed downstream at a sliver of bright green barely visible for all the blowing seed. The other canoe rounded a bend and disappeared from sight.

The wind died, and the Yukon wore a downy coat from bank to bank. Above the steep spruce-clad hills shooting out of the river, snow-streaked summits reared their bald heads.

Some hours later we came up on the gold camp at Fortymile, so named because it was forty miles downstream from Fort Reliance. We'd succeeded in putting all our competition behind us except the canoe. Our only stop had been a brief one, on a willowy gravel bar midstream. I answered the call of nature on one side of the bar and Jamie on the other. We ate a few hard biscuits and some dried fruit, then jumped back into the canoe.

We caught sight of the other Peterborough as it was making a stop on a tongue of land where the Yukon was joined by Fortymile Creek. A church steeple showed through the cottonwoods, as well as a Mountie post and a small cluster of log cabins. Nowadays it was a ghost town, but Fortymile had been a thriving gold camp three years before, when Dawson was nothing but an unnamed mud flat.

As the two men from the canoe were putting back in the river again, we floated up and paddled close for a friendly hello. Their canoe, I noticed, had a distinctive red arrow painted on the bow.

I was shocked to recognize the tall man in the stern from his handlebar mustache and granite face. The Sydney Mauler didn't recognize me. I wondered for a moment who his partner was. The man in the bow looked over his shoulder at me and grinned. I thought I might know him; I had to look twice. Though the rough-hewn clothing wasn't recognizable, the full beard and the sneer were. It was Cornelius Donner.

Burnt Paw, growling suddenly, recognized him too.

Donner said to his partner, "Sydney, I believe we've been overhauled by the Hawthorn pup and his vicious mastiff!"

"Donner and Brackett," I whispered to Jamie. "The two I told you about. Be on your guard."

"Hawthorn?" Brackett mumbled. "Any relation to Lucky Ethan Hawthorn?"

"He's the boxer's kid brother," Donner explained.

"Boxer? Human punching bag if you ask me."

"His kid brother here is more of a wrestler."

Brackett squinted at me. "Wrestler, eh? Could've fooled me."

"The girl must provide the power," Donner mocked. "How else could Hawthorn have caught us?"

"He must have told her this would be a picnic, Cornelius."

"Who *is* your partner, Hawthorn?"

"My name is Dunavant," Jamie broke in. "Jamie Dunavant. Say what you please, we aim to win."

"In which case," Donner snapped, "Hawthorn plans to give the prize money to me. Or hasn't he told you?"

"Why are *you* in the race?" I demanded of Donner. "Not for the money, certainly."

"For the glory of sport," Brackett answered instead, as his eyes, with detectable trepidation, scanned our Peterborough. "You mark my words—I won't be beat by a Hawthorn twice."

The canoes were starting to drift apart. I did nothing to lessen the gap.

Donner said, "You must think I'm a prophet, Hawthorn."

"Why do you say so?"

"Didn't I predict we'd meet down the Yukon, in Alaska? The border is only hours away."

"That was more like a threat, as I remember it."

"Oh no, you misunderstood. I must have been cautioning you about Alaska's lawless reputation. It's not like Canada, you know, with a Mountie behind every tree. From what I hear, half the Alaskans you meet are fleeing from the law. Maybe you should stick close to us, for protection."

Jamie scowled at them and started paddling.

"We can take care of ourselves," I said, and applied my own paddle. Burnt Paw yapped at them as we pulled away and took the lead.

They made no immediate push to catch us. They merely drifted with the current until we were out of sight.

"That was our canoe," Jamie said, her eyes welling up. "My father's and mine. Did you see the arrow drawn on the bow, in red?"

"I did."

"I painted that myself, after Father had written a poem entitled 'My Canoe Sings like an Arrow.' He sold the canoe shortly before we left for the States. When did those two scavengers descend on Dawson?"

"After you and your father left in July. I remember Ethan saying that Brackett arrived by steamboat shortly before ice-up. Donner got here by dogsled, around Christmas. Hired a team from Skagway."

"Father would turn over in his grave if we let ourselves get beaten by that canoe," Jamie said through gritted teeth. "If we keep them behind us from now on, that would suit me. They have more muscle, but they have to paddle their own weight, so it comes out even."

"Brackett doesn't seem quite right in the head," she added after a few minutes. "Too many punches, I bet. And Donner, he reminds me of the manager Father had the misfortune to hire to arrange our tour. J. P. Putnam was his name, or so he claimed—trustworthy as a viper."

"He sounds like a salesman for Dr. Kilmer's Swamp Root, Kidney, Liver and Bladder Cure."

"He could sell sand to Egyptians. My father was completely taken in. As it turned out, Putnam had been embezzling from us since San Francisco, where he leeched onto us. I suspected him for a thief, but Father would never look into our books. My father had no appetite for accounting. He was a typical Canadian frontiersman—honest as an elephant and possessing a child's faith in human nature."

"Honest as an elephant?"

"I've never met a dishonest elephant, have you? At any rate, Father assumed that every man he met was as honest as himself. When he died, I was left to deal with Putnam by myself. It was distressing—it was awful."

"What do you mean?"

"He proposed marriage to me."

"Marriage!" My breath caught short, I was so taken aback. I was boiling. "You don't mean it. The cad . . . and you were only fifteen!"

"I told him I planned to return to the North, as Father and I had told him right along. 'All of that's changed now,' he told me. 'I love you; I've loved you from the start. I see no reason why you shouldn't go on with the tour. We'll hire someone to play the part of your father—it's not a speaking part anyway.'"

"That weasel . . . I can hardly believe this!"

"Neither could I. And all of this only hours after I'd buried my father. I told Putnam that as far as his affections were concerned, I had in no way misled him. I'd never given him the slightest encouragement."

I was so relieved. My head reeled at the image of Jamie with this Putnam. I wanted to knock him down for even thinking of Jamie that way.

"In regard to the tour," Jamie said, "I told him I had no heart for giving voice to my father's poetry now that he was gone. 'Never mind that, then,' Putnam told me. 'You have a brilliant future as a dramatic actress.' I told him I'd heard that before, from well-wishers in every city we'd visited. 'Fame is your destiny!' he insisted. 'Only if I choose it,' I said. I told him that an actress is a bird in a gilded cage, and I'd rather have my freedom."

"It sounds like that's the way you truly feel."

"It is. I told him I might *write* for the stage one day, but he didn't want to hear about that. There was no money in that for him."

"You were to be his Sydney Mauler. That's why Donner reminded you of him."

"Exactly. Half an hour later it struck me like a bolt from heaven that Putnam was on his way to the bank. I caught him there, trying to withdraw the balance of our account. I asked the teller to call the police at once. Putnam fled on foot into the street. I never saw him again, thank goodness."

"You were all alone. What did you do? How did you manage?"

"I took a job in a laundry and moved in with the woman who owned it. She paid me extra to take her children to the park. The park was the only part of the city that appealed to me. I bided my time until late April, when I took the Great Northern to Seattle. All that time, I was thinking about the days getting longer in the North. I was like a Canada goose ready to fly home, believe me."

"Fancy dinners, fancy clothes, fancy people didn't suit you?"

"Look at the light reflecting off the Yukon, Jason— that's what suits me. Being with you again suits me. This glowing northern sky. That moose swimming the river downstream . . ."

Jamie was pointing. Sure enough, the branchlike object several hundred yards ahead was the antlers of a bull moose swimming for the left shore.

"All of this is what suits me."

We paddled close, so close I almost could have reached out and touched the animal's back. It was an immense bull with velveted antlers as wide as my outstretched arms.

Burnt Paw tried to stay as far away as he could manage without sliding off the far side of the canoe.

Movement slightly behind us caught my eye. Over my shoulder I was surprised to find the other Peterborough almost upon us. Donner's dark eyes were locked on the moose in the river.

A few seconds later and their canoe had slipped between us and the moose. Brackett, at the stern, reached for a rifle. "Moose steaks, mate!"

By this time we'd drifted thirty or forty feet away from them and the moose. Donner and Brackett were acting as if we weren't there, which suited me fine.

With the moose rolling its eyes back at them and swimming hard for the shore, the boxer seemed about to fire. Donner said, "That hardly seems sporting, Sydney. Let me see . . . paddle me close. Go on, do as I say."

My eyes met Jamie's. We had no idea what he was about to do.

"Closer, Sydney—right alongside."

Donner set his hat aside, peeled off his shirt, shucked his boots and his socks, and was making as if he was about to go over the side of the canoe. "Keep that rope handy."

Brackett looked just as baffled as we were. "Whatever you say, mate."

With one smooth motion, Donner was out of the canoe, into the chilly water, and onto the great moose's back. He had ahold of the antlers and was going for a ride!

"Yes sir!" Donner shouted. "Ride 'em, eh, Sydney?"

"He's a lunatic," I heard Jamie mutter.

The moose was fully aware of the man on his back, but there was nothing the animal could do about it. The whites of its eyes rolled back in fear and it shook its great antlers, but ineffectually.

It was then I saw Donner's right hand go to his hip, which was underwater. When his hand came back in view, it clutched a long-bladed sheath knife.

With his left hand Donner pulled himself onto the shoulders of the great beast, and with his right hand reaching around, he plunged the knife to the hilt in the moose's throat.

I gasped at the sight. The next I saw was a quick, fierce push with the knife hand.

The knife came out crimson. With an aborted groan and a wrenching wheeze, the moose was in the throes of death.

The river was turning red all around him as Donner swam for the canoe. "Lean the opposite way as I get in," he commanded of Brackett. After dropping his knife inside, Donner climbed hand-over-hand into the canoe.

Jamie and I watched dumbfounded as Donner ordered Brackett to paddle back to the moose. Donner was making ready a length of rope, which he proceeded to tie to the base of the antlers.

By this time we'd drifted well downstream of them, a hundred yards or more. Jamie was keeping us pointed upstream in order to see the conclusion of this strange stunt. We continued to drift, transfixed, as they paddled their prey to shore. "What kind of man is that, who would do such a thing for *sport*?" Jamie wondered aloud.

"Every time I see him, it gets worse."

We watched as they beached their canoe. Evidently they meant to stop, no doubt to build a fire and roast steaks. By this time the two were barely in sight upriver. We were close to shore, rounding a slight bend, losing sight of them. Suddenly Burnt Paw, looking downriver, perked up his ears and gave a strangled sort of warning bark.

Jamie and I swiveled around to look downstream and caught the fright of our lives. Extending far from the shore, to which it clung by its roots, was a living tree, a tremendous spruce tree lying on its side, sawing up and down in the river.

"Sweeper!" Jamie cried, and began to spin the canoe fast as she could. I helped with wide, shallow strokes until we were faced downstream, and then we both paddled with all our might.

Could we get around that sweeper?

I didn't think so. The tree was coming on nightmarishly fast. We couldn't reach the shore and we couldn't get around the tree.

"Not going to make it!" Jamie cried.

THIRTEEN

In every nerve of my body I knew this might be our death. The current was too strong, there was too little time. The big spruce loomed so close its branches seemed to fill the sky. What a foolish way to die, I thought, and then I realized that the sweeper itself was our only chance. I yelled, "Jump onto it!"

"Hit it broadside!" I heard Jamie yell back, and I felt her swinging the canoe around. For a moment I thought she was doing exactly the wrong thing, but then I understood—she was giving us both the chance to leap out.

The moment came in a dreamlike blur. As the tree was bobbing upward I rose, leapt onto the trunk, and grabbed a branch. I saw that Jamie—thank God—had done the same, saw the canoe below us pinned against the sweeper and tipping on its side, saw Burnt Paw leap at the last moment onto the trunk between us.

His claws scratched for a hold and they caught, but it

was apparent he wasn't going to be able to withstand the rocking-horse motion for long. Working my way toward him, I snatched him up with my free hand. Jamie clung tight to a branch and reached into the surging white water for her paddle, which was riding up and down against the trunk of the tree. Mine was nowhere to be seen.

As the tree trunk was on an upswing, I noticed huge branches sticking straight down into the river. I shuddered to realize that one of us could have been pinned underwater, impossible to reach, against those branches.

The canoe, at times mostly underwater and at times mostly above, was on its side with its hull facing upstream in a froth of white water. It was pinned against the sweeper with a tremendous amount of force. Branches spoking underneath the canoe kept it from being swept under the tree. I wondered if there was any way to get at our gear or to free the canoe.

"The tree could turn loose of the bank!" Jamie shouted over her shoulder. She was already working her way along the trunk toward the shore. It was a gradual climb, but upright branches along the route provided secure holds to counter the up-and-down motion of the tree. I followed with Burnt Paw, hoping the sweeper's roots wouldn't lose their grip on the bank before we could get there.

Up ahead, Jamie was stopped. The last fifteen or twenty feet had no limbs at all and would have to be walked like an inclined tightrope. Fortunately the trunk was massive and the tightrope wide.

"It's barely rocking at this end," Jamie reported.

Paddle in hand, she negotiated the crossing. At the last she climbed to the bank across the largest of the roots. I held my breath and followed with the dog, and then I collapsed in the grass beside Jamie. Burnt Paw was in a frenzy, dancing around us and licking our faces.

"I know, Burnt Paw," Jamie told him, fighting tears. "We're very lucky to be alive."

"You did well," I said. "If you hadn't—"

"Jason," she corrected me, "I'll never forgive myself. I can't believe I let this happen!"

"We both let it happen."

"I was in the stern."

"We're safe, that's all that counts."

"It's not like I didn't know to be on guard for sweepers. I just couldn't keep my eyes off those two and the moose. It was all so strange. I just didn't think."

"Think of it this way: All that I can tell we lost is your hat."

Her hand went to her head. "I didn't even notice."

"The canoe," I said, struggling to my feet. "There's an awful lot of current holding it. Looks impossible to work it around the tip of the tree."

She nodded her agreement.

"Maybe if it were empty—if we could pull everything out of it. It's a wonder it isn't broken."

With a rueful laugh, Jamie said, "It's Canadian-made."

"Look how well anchored the tree is. A lot more bank would have to wash away before it turns loose. We could go back and forth . . . unload the canoe one piece of gear at a time."

"If we were extremely careful, maybe we could."

"We could get back in the race."

Jamie's face flashed red and tears welled. "We could have lost our lives! We still could, out there. Don't even think about the race!"

Abashed, I could see it. If we rushed, we were going

to get hurt or killed. "You're right," I said, and I meant it. "We don't have to win the race, but we still want to go to Nome, don't we, and get there on our own?"

"That we do." She was still angry with me.

"We'll be as cautious as can be. What if I'm tied to a short piece of rope? We can use the bow rope . . . short enough so I couldn't fall in. I could hand things to you, and you could work them to shore one piece at a time."

Jamie brushed her tears away. "It might work." A moment later, full of determination, she said, "Let's try it."

With Burnt Paw barking from the shore, we went back out on the sweeper and began to pick our way through its branches toward the canoe.

Burnt Paw wasn't barking any longer. I turned around, half afraid he was following us. Indeed, he was practically at my heels. "Get back!" I yelled at him. "Don't you remember it's a bucking horse out there?"

The rocking motion was already such that he didn't need convincing. Burnt Paw ran back along the trunk to shore, then started barking up and down the bank.

"Now it almost looks like he wants to swim to us," Jamie said.

"He's not that crazy," I assured her.

A second later, on the downstream side of the sweeper, the mutt leapt into the river and swam twenty or more feet into the calm water down there before he turned around and paddled for shore.

"He's got something in his mouth," Jamie reported.

"What in the world?"

Burnt Paw came onto shore and shook himself out, still hanging on to some crumpled black object.

"My hat!" Jamie exclaimed. "He's rescued my hat!"

Burnt Paw wagged that bent tail of his as we praised

him for being a hero. Making our way out to the canoe, we found it still unscathed. We'd lashed the oilskin tarp well enough that so far none of our gear had escaped. The shotgun was still held by the ropes—barely. With my free hand I reached down to untie the bow line that we were going to use for my safety rope. "This is all going to take a lot of doing," I said, and as I spoke, my eyes caught a motion out across the river and slightly upstream—rowed boats, a dozen or more, pulling hard.

"*What* race?" I said with a laugh.

In the hours to come, every single skiff and scow passed us by. Those who floated by close enough to see us mostly quit rowing, stopped and stared, then started rowing again as they passed us by. We understood. They were in a race with so many contestants it could be decided by seconds. Some, nevertheless, hollered out, "Are you okay?" or "Do you need help?" We hollered back, "Thank you! We're okay!" and watched them go by. In truth, more people on the sweeper would be dangerous.

At the very end of the parade came the green canoe. Strange, but I'd forgotten that Donner and Brackett even existed.

At first they just stared at us, assessing our situation. Then the boxer yelled, "Hey, Hawthorn, the river's half a mile wide! Crafty boating, mate, crafty boating!"

I felt like telling him and his bloodthirsty partner to consign themselves to eternal hellfire, but I held my tongue. So, I noticed, did Donner. Even from a distance of thirty yards I was chilled by his calculating stare.

In the twilight between eleven and one we were still working. The sun was rising as we pulled the canoe out of the water and onto the trunk of the tree. We tied on with our long rope, floated the canoe on the downstream side of the tree, then bit by bit passed our end around the branches as we worked it to shore.

We wrung every drop of water we could from our sodden clothes and bedrolls, then spread them out to the sun on racks we improvised from driftwood. Inventorying our foodstuffs, we separated what could be salvaged from what was ruined. We set our dried fruits, jerked meats, and bacon out to dry and counted our flour, baking powder, biscuits, and dried vegetables a complete loss. There would be a trading post at the Alaska gold camp of Eagle City, just across the border, where we could at least buy bannock makings—flour and baking powder—with our last five dollars.

Fortunately we had a quantity of tinned foods, mostly salmon. We had our knives, the saw and the ax, our tarp and our tent. The match safe had kept our matches dry. All we'd lost to the river had been my canoe paddle, and thanks to Jamie's foresight, we had the spare.

We counted ourselves extremely lucky.

Lucky and exhausted. We spread out the oilskin tarp, threw ourselves down on it, and slept, no matter that the sun was bright and the new day already warming at three in the morning.

Approaching wakefulness, I heard bacon hissing on a stove. Abe is already cooking breakfast, I thought, and I'm not even up. I'll be late for the mill.

The next thing I heard was the chuffing of a steam engine. The engine at the mill, I figured. Someone else has stoked the furnace, and I was supposed to have done it.

My eyes opened to a vast expanse of water and bluffs in the distance. Amid my confusion, the foreground exploded with motion. A flock of red-breasted ducks rose from the water and ran skittering along the surface, their black-and-white wings beating a frenzy until they rose, all at once, into the air.

As I blinked away the onslaught of the light I realized I was on the Yukon River with Jamie. I rolled over—there she was, sound asleep. I heard the swooshing sound of the sweeper sawing up and down in the river and remembered what had happened.

I got up and stretched, looking out across the river and upstream.

What I saw dumbfounded me. In the middle of the vast Yukon River, in broad daylight, floated a two-story building.

FOURTEEN

I dropped to my knees and shook Jamie by the shoulder. Her eyes popped open as if she were in mortal peril. "Whaa—" she started to say.

"Sorry to wake you, but there's something out on the river that you have to see."

She got to her knees, blinking away the light, and shaded her eyes. "What in the world?"

The building was close enough now that I could make out the lettering between the first and second stories: MOONLIGHT HOTEL.

"The Moonlight, from Dawson!" Jamie exclaimed.

The next moment the letters began to turn away from us. The chuffing of a steam engine carried across the water—the same sound I thought I'd dreamed. Suddenly we could see that the hotel was on a small barge being pushed by a tiny sternwheeler.

Jamie rubbed her eyes. "But what's it doing here?"

"Moving to St. Michael?" I guessed. "Nome?"

With a yawn, Jamie lay down on her back and fetched her watch out of her trouser pocket. She yawned again and opened it up. "Ten before eight. We've lost . . . almost fifteen hours."

"But we're no longer in a hurry," I reminded her.

She sat upright, suddenly alert and conspiratorial. "There's a long way to go. A lot could happen. Who says we can't still win?"

Here came Burnt Paw between us with a flurry of kisses that sent Jamie bounding to her feet like a colt off to the races. "Jason, our bedrolls are dry! Let's roll them up and put them away! Hurry!"

We waved to the two men at the rail of the little stern-wheeler, the *New Racket*. A third waved from the wheelhouse.

On a whim, Jamie flew to picking wildflowers from the profusion around us—blue lupine, goldenrod, and pink shooting stars. In the next instant she was running in a circle around the tarp and tossing the colors into the air. Burnt Paw was beside himself chasing after her, barking, leaping to catch the flowers.

"I'm so happy to be alive!" she cried.

Jamie's dark hair had fallen out of its braid, and now it danced, fetching and disheveled, on her shoulders. "Father and I stayed in the Moonlight Hotel when we first arrived in Dawson! Jason, it's a good luck sign, don't you think?"

"I do, I do," I said, feeling merry as she.

"Let me tell you a joke," Jamie said breathlessly, coming to a sudden stop. She seemed to have forgotten we were in a hurry, but then, so had I.

"You ever hear about the two prospectors who were walking along the railroad track when they spied a human arm lying off to the side?"

I shook my head.

"'That looks like Pete's arm,' said the first prospector. 'It is Pete's arm,' said the second."

I couldn't help but chuckle. This was already funny.

"They walked on a little ways and then they saw a human leg beside the rails. 'That looks like Pete's leg,' observed the first prospector. 'It *is* Pete's leg,' said the second. After a short while they saw a head lying beside the track. 'That looks like Pete's head,' said the first prospector. 'It *is* Pete's head,' replied the second prospector, who stooped and picked it up. He held it by the ears, gave it a shake, and cried, 'Pete, are you hurt?'"

I'd been trying not to bust out laughing, and now I could. Ethan-like, I slapped myself on my thigh so hard it hurt. Burnt Paw was so excited he was springing up eye level with me again and again as if he had steel coils in his little feet.

"Yep, Jamie," I said, "that's sure-enough funny. Got any more?"

"Maybe so," she said, suddenly serious. Her eyes were surveying the disorder all around us. "But we have to get packed!"

"Just one more?"

"Later, on the river . . . if you're good, both of you."

We were back on the river little more than an hour when we saw the sign at the border: ENTERING ALASKA. Before long we passed under the Indian village of Eagle, a jumble of cabins atop a cutbank on our left. Dressed-out salmon from pink to the color of cured tobacco decorated drying racks all along the bluff. Close to river level, sled dogs appeared out of holes they'd dug in the banks to keep cool. Each was chained to a stake. As we floated by, some barked and some howled like wolves until we were far down the river.

Twenty minutes later we made our stop at the tiny mining town of Eagle City, fast as we could, for flour and baking powder. The gold camp was up on a high bluff above a spectacular horseshoe bend in the river; we took a second leaving the trading post to admire the view. The *Hannah*, one of the Alaska Commercial Company's new steamboats, was just arriving from downriver.

We raced down the hill. The *Hannah*'s passengers spilling onto the dock were on their way to Dawson, but they were all buzzing about the Great Race, which must have been a colorful sight for them indeed. We took no time to ask who was in the lead but put back on the river as fast as we could.

Below Eagle City we entered a deep twisting canyon with sheer bluffs on the curves. We passed the mouths of four rivers entering from the north—the Seventymile, the Tatunduk, the Nation, and the Kandik. At last I reminded Jamie that I'd been very, very good, and she said, "I thought you'd never mention it. You keep paddling. Did you hear about the two prospectors who went duck hunting? The first one shot, and when a duck fell out of the sky he said how terrible he felt about it being dead. The second prospector said, 'Don't feel so bad— the fall would've killed him anyway.'"

I kept paddling, but I sure had a good laugh.

From behind me came her animated voice. "What about the prospector bride who cried her eyes out when her husband went out with all the other prospectors to shoot craps? She didn't know how to cook them."

I gave the Yukon a slap with my paddle, which set off Burnt Paw barking.

"Did you hear about the prospectors building a

house? One of them went to the boss and asked if they should build it from the bottom up or the top down. The boss yelled at him, 'Start from the bottom and build up, you numbskull!' The prospector turned to his partners and said, 'Rip 'er down, boys! Gotta start over!'"

I turned around and said, "I just hope you have more, or I'll throw myself in the river."

She shrugged. "I don't, so go ahead."

"On second thought, I won't. Where did you get them?"

"I heard them in another form last winter. I turned them into prospector jokes and worked them into a play I wrote."

"You've written a *play*? You don't mean it."

Neither of us was paddling now. "I wrote it on my voyage north to pass the time. I finished it as we were pulling into St. Michael, and did some polishing on the journey up the river. I gave it to Arizona Charlie before we left. Maybe he's read it by now. I wrote it with his Palace Grand in mind."

"What's the play about?"

"It's about Dawson City—it's a satire on the rise of the kings of the Klondike. Guess who I patterned it on? It's entitled *The Adventures of Big Olaf McDoughnut*."

"Big Alex McDonald!"

"None other. I'm guessing that Dawson City audiences will love a Klondike story. As for Big Alex, I met him last year—he won't mind fun being poked his way. In fact, he might die laughing; he's known for being generous."

"I can swear to that. Do you remember my companion of last summer, Charlie Maguire? We wintered at Five Fingers together, canoed into Dawson together?"

"I remember Charlie. He'd lost one leg at the knee."

"That's him. Charlie wanted to get home to Chicago, and we were saving up money for the transportation. Big Alex found out and invited him to stuff his pockets from a bowl full of nuggets."

"I didn't know that! That will be perfect for the story, and I can picture just the spot for it. I'll write a part for Charlie into the play. . . . The scene with the bowl of nuggets will come near the end. There's a certain spot that's been nagging at me that needs a lift."

"You're a writer, Jamie. A writer!"

"Just a cobbler of words . . . I'm my father's daughter."

"Will Arizona Charlie pay you for your play, if he likes it, which I know he will?"

"Five hundred dollars for a year's permission, and fifty dollars for every performance."

"Imagine!"

"We shook on it."

After a break on shore to ease our aching backs and eat a quick meal, we turned to hard paddling and putting on some miles. Hour after hour went by without us catching sight of a single race boat. We passed a few Indian fish camps.

At sunset, around eleven, we went to shore to stretch our legs and eat a bite or two. When we set off again, I was in the stern. Jamie stretched out on the gear in front of me. With one hand under her head and the other curled around Burnt Paw, she said softly, "Our canoe sings like an arrow." A minute later she was sound asleep.

Paddling at the stern with Jamie asleep so peacefully in front of me, the dog curled against her shoulder, the broad, empty sweep of the Yukon ahead, I was filled with the greatest contentment I had ever known.

"Being with you again suits me," I remembered her

saying. "All of this is what suits me."

Being with Jamie, seeing all this grand country for the first time—I couldn't have asked for more, unless it was to get back in the race. All night I kept paddling hard.

It must have been around six in the morning, with Jamie recently roused and paddling again, that we caught sight of the Moonlight Hotel and the *New Racket*, the pint-sized relic of a sternwheeler that was pushing it. We soon realized that the pair was moored at the landing of the most famous town in the interior of Alaska, Circle City.

Circle City's surroundings offered little to please the eye. The mountains had fallen behind, and the river sprawled more than a mile wide here, dirty and yellow and resembling a broad lake.

We needed a stretch and a few minutes off the river. Upstream of the boat dock, we tied up to a leaning black spruce and climbed the low bluff for a look at the celebrated gold camp turned ghost town.

The names of dozens of saloons and dance halls had faded on their disintegrating facades. Some couldn't be read. The sod roofs of a few of the log cabins had fallen in; doors were mostly boarded up on cabins and commercial buildings alike. Two saloons, the Midnight Sun and the Last Chance, had new paint, and so did Mae's Roadhouse across the street.

Only three years before, Circle had been a thriving town of more than a thousand, but that was before the big strike on the Klondike that gave rise to Dawson. The most famous thing about Circle City these days was its mistaken moniker. When they named the town they thought it was on the Arctic Circle, but it turned out that the sun refused to cooperate at midsummer and stay above the horizon around the clock. It set briefly, even on June 21. To see the sun above the horizon at midnight, to actually reach the Arctic Circle, you had to float fifty miles farther north.

As we walked along the bank, the mosquitoes found us. This far downriver it was always just a matter of time once we were on land—seconds, usually. Fortunately, the devils weren't very numerous or bloodthirsty at the moment. We were able to walk along the riverbank for a closer look at the crumbling town and the floating hotel from Dawson that had stopped for a visit.

A husky from a team tied outside one of the cabins started to bark at Burnt Paw, but when the others didn't join in, it quit.

"Looks like no one's around the dock," Jamie said. "The crew from the *New Racket* must have laid over here for the night. I sure would like to peek inside the Moonlight. We'll be quick."

We walked up the gangplank to the *New Racket* and along its rails. The crew wasn't around. "Sleeping in the hotel or up at the roadhouse," Jamie guessed. "I'm curious to see if the Moonlight ever got fixed up."

"I don't think I've ever been in it."

"The walls were mostly wallpaper over canvas—the hotel was one of the first in Dawson and was patched together with whatever was around. If somebody was snoring upstairs and two rooms down the hall, it sounded like the trumpet of doom!"

From the bow of the little sternwheeler we stepped onto the barge that floated the hotel. The front door had been removed. We walked into the lobby.

A mural over the registration desk caught my eye. It was entitled "Moonlight on the Yukon." It was a winter scene with the light of the full moon glinting off snow-covered mountains and the frozen river. My eye was drawn to a speck of a lonely cabin in the corner of the painting with golden lamplight showing through frosted windows. A delicate plume of smoke wafted from the chimney. A closer look revealed snowshoe tracks leading to the front door. Everything about the scene had me awash in memories. It was as if I'd made those tracks myself, returning to the cabin after an unsuccessful moose hunt downriver. Charlie and I were inside that cabin slowly starving on half rations.

From the corner of my eye I saw Burnt Paw perk up his ears. Jamie scooped him up with one arm, caught my eye, and nodded toward the hallway.

Burnt Paw's eyes also swiveled toward the hallway. I heard two voices, one with an English accent. No, Australian. Was it Brackett?

Yes, and the other was Donner.

FIFTEEN

"You said we could afford to loaf a little," came the boxer's irritable voice.

"You slept seven hours," Donner barked. "Whenever we're off the river the competition gets farther ahead, or haven't you figured that out?"

"I'd rather go ten rounds in the ring than ten hours in that torture device you call a canoe."

I wondered why we hadn't seen their canoe at the riverbank. Had they pulled it out of sight in the willows?

"Those blighters on the bleeding scows . . . they have it easy, eh? Stretch out and enjoy the ride. At least we could have taken a rowboat."

"Too heavy for the shortcut," Donner snapped. "I already told you that."

"It's all third-hand, third-hand. You heard it off a fellow who heard it off a stoker on a steamboat. An Indian, to boot. I wouldn't trust an aborigine, I wouldn't."

"Nonetheless, our canoe is the fastest thing on the river, just as I told you it would be. You've had your rest, now let's get going. We have a lot of catching up to do."

"Our canoe would be faster yet aboard this hotel, eh? Stash it out of sight? We could ride in comfort all the way to St. Michael. What do you say?"

"I say we'd be found out. We're in this to win."

"Back in Dawson you said it was for the glory of sport! You're a wealthy man, Donner. Half the prize money would be a spit in your bucket."

"What I brought with me won't get us past Nome."

"You mean back to Dawson."

"I'm not thinking about Dawson, I'm thinking about Australia. What do you say to a fighting tour of your home country? You'd be a conquering hero, surely. How long has it been?"

"It's been years, but what in blazes are you talking about?"

"I heard there's a regular fleet of ships anchored off Nome. Ships coming and going all the time. As soon as we get there and collect our prize, we'll board the first one south."

"And leave all your assets behind in Dawson? Are you daft?"

There was a silence. When the reply came, it was in a grave tone. "There's a *fiend* after me, Sydney. A bloodhound."

Jamie might have shifted her weight, or else the floorboard just happened to creak.

"What's that?" Donner said.

We both held our breath. I could only hope they didn't hear the beating of my heart.

"This wreck creaking, that's all," Brackett said finally. "What's this about a bloodhound after you?

You're speaking in riddles."

"A detective is after me. There, is that clear enough? I thought I'd shaken him last August in Kansas City. I saw him yesterday at the rail of the *Hannah*, heading upriver. He studied us both like a hawk, but he didn't recognize me in this garb, under this beard—all he has is a photograph of my former self. And another name, of course. He's on his way to Dawson. I can't go back there."

There was a lengthy pause. We were in a dangerous situation. A glance at Jamie, and her eyes rolled toward our path of escape.

"Why? What's he after you for?" came the boxer's hoarse whisper.

"A fire in Omaha—a business I owned—a man died."

"You're wanted for arson and murder?"

"As God is my witness, Sydney, I had nothing to do with it."

That was the last we heard. We ghosted outside and tiptoed along the rail of the *New Racket* and across the gangplank to the shore. With a glance over my shoulder I satisfied myself that we weren't being followed. Then the huskies up at that cabin started barking, every last one of them. We ran.

A few minutes later we were back in our canoe and paddling a wide arc around the little sternwheeler and the Moonlight Hotel. To my dismay, Donner and Brackett were outside the hotel now, by the front door. And they were staring at us.

We didn't say a word, just kept paddling.

They didn't call, they didn't wave, they just stood there like granite.

Jamie and I didn't speak until we'd slipped into the labyrinth of sloughs and channels of the island-studded

Yukon Flats. "They don't seem to be following," I whispered. Sound, I knew, carries uncannily far over water.

"Do they suspect we overheard them?" Jamie fretted.

"They might. Donner must suspect his own shadow."

"We have to be watchful. We have to stay out of their way."

"Agreed," I said, swatting at a sudden swarm of mosquitoes. They had descended on us with a vengeance.

Now that the Yukon was fingering its way among a welter of islands, we couldn't paddle to the center of the river to get away from them. Quick as we might, we pulled on our head nets and reached for our gloves.

Safe despite the whine and the buzz, I started to talk faster than I could think. "A fire in Omaha—a business he owned—a man died. Donner—or whatever his name really is—was the co-owner of the Bodega Saloon in Dawson, Jamie, along with the man who died in the fire. Watson, his name was. When Watson died, Donner became the *sole* owner. The great fire this April started upstairs in the Bodega Saloon!"

"How?"

"They thought it was an accident. The bartender carried Watson upstairs, dead drunk, and put him in his bed. The Mounties concluded that Watson must have roused himself enough to light a candle in a block of wood, then fell unconscious again."

"You don't suppose Donner was in the saloon when his partner was carried upstairs. . . ."

"I *know* he was. I was on the street outside when Donner came out yelling 'Fire!' When the bartender returned downstairs, Donner must have slipped upstairs and lit the candle, knowing what would happen. First he lit the fire, then he announced it!"

"You know what, I'll bet anything it was a *partner*

of Donner's who died in the fire in Omaha. The detective will discover the pattern. That's why Donner can't go back to Dawson. I wonder if he was seen going upstairs. . . . I bet he had the Bodega Saloon insured."

"He did. He rebuilt it."

"The detective will find out that Cornelius Donner hasn't been seen in Dawson since—"

"Since the day that the race started! And the names of Donner and Brackett will appear on the Alaska Commercial Company's records. That bloodhound Donner is worried about will turn around and track him downriver."

"The question is, By the time the detective figures all this out, can he get to Nome before Donner does? He might have to track him to Australia."

"Here's another question, Jamie. Did you hear Donner mention a shortcut? If he really knows one, how is anyone—including us—going to get to Nome before he does? Where could that shortcut be?"

"Around the mouth of the Yukon? Close to the ocean, the river splits into so many channels, maybe the fastest route can be navigated only by canoe. Maybe you can only reach it by carrying the canoe on a portage path. I only wish I knew!"

The river continued to unravel within the vast swamp called the Flats. It was impossible to tell side channels from the main channel because there was no main channel. Our map was useless. We were definitely not making eight miles an hour anymore—far from it. The Flats were an immensely complicated web of moving water, sloughs, ponds, and islands, all teeming with life. We saw moose browsing belly-deep for greenery growing from the bottom and black bears swimming the river. A humpbacked grizzly rose from the blueberries, stood, and squinted at us as we passed silently by. Tens of thousands of geese, ducks, and cranes were on the water and in the sky.

Untold billions of mosquitoes tempered our enjoyment of this wild pageant. They rose from the muskeg swamps and swarmed upon us like a biblical plague.

I would have expected little current in a section of the river called the Flats, but the current was relentless, furious at times. The whirlpools that formed where channels converged, sometimes three channels at once, would have tipped us over if we hadn't braced and paddled our way carefully through them.

The river swept us across sixty-six and one-half degrees, north latitude: the Arctic Circle. We knew it had happened when midnight next came. At midnight, the sun dipped near the horizon, danced along it, then rose. It never set, but instead continued on its great circle around the sky. We prayed for wind to drive the mosquitoes away, and our prayers were answered with booming thunder and a storm that had us donning all the wool we'd brought and our oilskin raincoats in addition.

The storm kept coming and we kept paddling. We were overtaking boats now, always with a glance over the shoulder for the other Peterborough which, gratefully, we never spied. We passed Fort Yukon, the biggest Indian village on the river and consequently the biggest trading post, without a stop. In a driving rain we could barely make out its cabins and the wide Porcupine River coming in from the northeast.

Sometimes the wind came in gusts and lifted sheets of water off the river and drove it in our faces. I'd bail with a coffee can, fast as I could, while Jamie at the stern kept paddling. Sometimes the water turned so violent we were in danger of swamping, and we had to go to shore and huddle under the stunted timber.

In between the squalls the weather improved, still cloudy but with a steady breeze that kept the mosquitoes at bay. We were desperate for a warm meal, and at the mouth of the Chandalar I shot a goose. To our great surprise Burnt Paw leapt from the canoe and proved himself a retriever of more than hats, no matter that the goose was bigger than he was. We took the time to make a fire and cook. We warmed ourselves with tea, picked blueberries, and made a bannock cake in the skillet. Nests were everywhere. We added fried eggs to our feast and hard-boiled dozens for later. Afterward we bathed separately at the bank, behind the willows.

The storm kept coming, yet we put back on the river. We had to stay especially vigilant on these floodwaters because there were not only sweepers clinging to the banks, but numbers of trees washing right down the river. Several times we witnessed the Yukon in the act of undermining its cutbanks and toppling tall cottonwoods.

In the midst of a downpour, Jamie told me, "I wouldn't trade this adventure for all the gold in the Klondike and Nome put together."

"What can the river throw at us that it hasn't already?" I replied.

"Don't ask!"

Since Fort Yukon, the river had been swinging to the southwest. When the storm cleared we found ourselves below the Arctic Circle once again. For half an hour around midnight the sun hid behind the horizon and a luminous arctic glow filled the sky. The same glow filled my heart. I loved that girl more than I could ever say. I'd never felt so *alive*.

It had been three or four days since Circle City—

we'd lost track—and we knew we must be bound to leave the Flats soon. The river was still a maze of channels and islands, sloughs and sweepers. We were eager to have the Yukon come together again.

At one of the countless places where the waters branched, we could see, to our left a quarter mile or more away and off on a minor channel, a scow that had been beached on the upriver end of a gravel island by the receding water. We could make out a man and a woman knee-deep in the river and struggling with long poles to lever their scow free. On the scow, two small children stood by the entrance of the tent and watched.

Suddenly the man and the woman spied us. The man climbed onto the scow, snatched up a rifle, and began to fire shots into the air. Immediately, Jamie tried to swerve the canoe in the direction of the channel where they'd run aground, while I added sweeping stokes to try to make the turn. We kept struggling, but the current in our channel was overpowering and swept us past the entrance to theirs. We were swept around the right side of a large island covered with cottonwoods that separated the two channels.

"Do you think we can get to them—give them a hand?" I yelled to Jamie, and she hollered back, "Let's try."

We paddled for shore and beached the canoe on the island, tied it securely, and scrambled for what might prove helpful: ax, saw, and our hundred-foot coil of spare rope.

Just as we were about to start into the woods, here came the green canoe shooting by, with the murderer in the bow, the boxer in the stern. The starch had gone out of the Mauler's handlebar mustache.

Perhaps out of awkwardness, the fright that came

with seeing them, I raised my hand and gave them a wave. With no wave in return, the two stared at us as they passed, then resumed paddling. They were soon out of sight.

We hesitated, knowing we could lose hours here. I was shaking with frustration. "There's no justice if those two win," I said, "but that family over there needs us."

"Forget those scoundrels," Jamie said. "We may not be able to get over to that scow once we cross this island, but we can try. We have to try."

SIXTEEN

The island proved to be hundreds of yards wide. The crossing was painfully slow through a morass of drift-piles, muck, rock, forest, mosquitoes, and muskeg. At last we were on the far side. We walked up the shore until we were opposite the scow. The family on the other side of the swift-running channel was surprised to see us. It had been an hour since they'd fired the shots, and we'd passed from view. The woman had changed from her dress into shirt and trousers.

We were separated by seventy-five feet of rushing water, but it was no more than knee-deep from the look of it. Jamie and I clasped hands, and we started across.

"Ve tank you," cried the man and the woman, with deep emotion, as we waded alongside their scow. Jamie had crossed with Burnt Paw in one arm. She set him down on the scow, much to the delight of two big-eyed children, a boy and a girl, three and five years old from appearances. Burnt Paw wagged his bent tail and let them very cautiously and delicately pet him.

Like their parents, the children were round-faced and blond. The little girl, like her mother, wore her hair in pigtails.

"Ve much tankful," said the man, who wasn't much older than Abe. "I make a bad judgment back der. Most of vater going right, but dis scow, she seemed to vant to go dis vay and I tought, 'Let her go.'"

"Ve been here hours," the woman explained. "Vait for vater to come back up—maybe it not gonna."

"Are you from Germany?" Jamie asked.

"From Svee-den," the woman replied.

"Are you in the race to Nome, like us?"

"Ve hear about race," the man said, "from some a dese people ve see, but ve not race. Ve try to get up Koyukuk River before vinter."

"Before fall, Johan," his wife corrected him.

"Ve go five hunnert mile up Koyukuk River. Past Arctic Circle. Get some moose, make a cabin, let it snow!"

I asked, "Is there gold up there?"

"Not so much. Ve jes vant to go live der. Prettiest place in whole vorld—I been der, got to go back with Ingrid."

Jamie's hazel eyes were sparkling. "I think I remember seeing the Koyukuk where it comes into the Yukon. It runs clear, doesn't it?"

The man beamed a golden smile. "Five hunnert mile, clear as glass. Birch, big spruce, pine, bootiful mountains . . . moose, vild sheep, caribou, salmon, garten in summer, mebbe a little gold to buy supplies, couple Indian villages. Everybody friendly, no matter vat kind of people dey are, valk a hunnert mile to help you even in vinter. Dat's paradise on dis earth, up dat Koyukuk River."

Jamie and I looked at each other. I know what I was thinking. Maybe we should be going up that Koyukuk River with these Swedes.

We shook their hands and introduced ourselves.

"Let's see if we can help get you unstuck and on your way to your Koyukuk River," Jamie offered.

The scow was weighed down by a family's outfit for a year: tools and clothing, flour and sugar and dried grub of all descriptions. After cutting two more poles, we tried to lever the scow free, all four of us, but we couldn't budge it.

The only thing to be done was to unweight the scow. We set to work wading the supplies a hundred feet to dry ground. It was going to take a long time.

Not long after we started the unloading, I thought I heard the sound of ax blows in the distance. Standing in loud rushing water, I couldn't be sure. Some stampeder making firewood, I supposed, if it was anything at all. The sound came and went, and then it was gone altogether. I didn't give it another thought.

At last everything had been removed from the Swedes' scow except the family's canvas wall tent and their Yukon stove. The kids and Burnt Paw watched as Jamie, Ingrid, and I bent our backs to the poles while Johan, roped to the scow and out in front, pulled like an ox toward open water.

We budged it, then we budged it half a dozen more times, and finally the big floating platform of logs decked over with milled lumber came free. Johan jumped on and manned the big sweep oar, keeping the scow out in the current as it bumped and scraped its way into deeper water. I snatched the tie rope, and the rest of us ran alongside in the shallows. Several hundred yards downriver we managed to beach the brute of a craft on a gravel spit that speared out into deep water.

Then came the last of the ordeal. Piece by piece, we began to carry their outfit down the long cobbled beach. Ingrid and Johan begged us to rejoin our race, but they were in a race more urgent than ours—with winter— and we wanted to see them safely on their way. By now we'd learned that our friends, the Swensons, were hoping to catch a small steamboat that served the villages up the Koyukuk. The steamboat made the upriver run from the Yukon only once a summer, before the Koyukuk became too shallow for navigation, and that would be soon. If they missed the steamboat, their dream was at an end.

When we were done, Ingrid gave us a gunnysack of groceries, including several fresh bannock cakes baked with berries they'd picked. They made us promise to come find them up the Koyukuk one day so they could repay our kindness properly. I heard us both saying that we would.

At last we were able to push the Swensons off and wish them luck. We hadn't realized it, but Burnt Paw was on the scow playing with the kids. Now that the scow was in motion, he raced back and forth across the deck, looking from the kids to us and back as if trying to make up his mind. I shouted, "It's up to you, Burnt Paw!"

I'm not sure what it was that decided him. Maybe it was having heard how far north they were headed—his shorthaired coat was even less suited for the Koyukuk than it was for Dawson City. At any rate, Burnt Paw leapt into the shallow river and paddled his way to shore.

We felt awful good wading the channel, returning to the big island, and tramping back to the canoe. We were imagining what that upper Koyukuk River would look like. In my mind I was felling trees and building a log cabin.

When we cleared the cottonwoods and first caught sight of our canoe, it didn't add up, what our eyes took in. It just couldn't be.

Our hearts were in our throats. It just couldn't be.

The canoe was under a tree, destroyed. The fallen trunk of a tall cottonwood had crushed it and cleaved it in two.

Our eyes went to the freshly hewn stump of the cottonwood. There were bright white chips all around its base and gum boot tracks everywhere in the mud.

"How could they have done this?" Jamie cried.

I was too stunned, too angry to speak. Two pairs of tracks along the shore led from downstream and returned in the same direction.

"They heard the gunshots," Jamie said. "They saw the family in trouble, saw we'd stopped to help them."

"And then they did this!" I stormed. Through tears of rage, I said, "Jamie, I don't think we can salvage the canoe."

"We can't," she agreed, unsuccessfully fighting back tears of her own.

We looked up and down the river. We were utterly alone.

"It's a matter of time before someone uses this channel," I said. "Someone will come along. Donner and Brackett did."

"They might have been *following* us down this channel. We haven't been looking behind us."

"No, we haven't."

"There are so many channels besides this one, we might be stuck here." Jamie's eyes fell on the broken canoe and our gear crushed under the trunk of the cottonwood. With a rueful laugh, she added, "Right now maybe I *would* trade this adventure for the combined gold of Nome and the Klondike."

"We may be out of the race," I said, "but we aren't maimed or dead. That's something, I suppose."

A grim smile crossed her face. "I don't know if it was a shred of decency, or if it was because they were in a hurry, but at least they didn't take the time to destroy our gear. If this tree has broken any of our hard-boiled eggs I'm going to be *really* furious."

Her smile forced one of my own. "Our canoe paddles are missing, but we've got all our tools—saw and ax, knives, rope, canvas, even some nails." I was thinking hard, casting around for solutions. My eyes went upstream to a huge driftpile at the head of the island. I studied it closely—there were a number of splendid logs up there not that badly entangled.

Jamie's eyes had followed mine. "A log raft?"

"We could make a couple of sweep oars and row standing up. For blades, we could saw a couple of three-foot sections from the canoe. Then we could nail and lash them to a couple of thin, stout poles—"

"There'll be some alder or birch in that driftpile. You know, Jason, as long as we don't ride on a boat with someone else, we're still in the race. You never know what could happen. Maybe the opportunity will come along to exchange our raft for Father's canoe. They think they're so much faster than anyone else that they can afford to sleep on shore."

"We'll keep our eyes open. Wouldn't that be something!"

We worked all night, not that night ever came. Twice we stopped to make coffee, eat the bannock cakes Ingrid had given us, and inspect our progress. When our raft came together it was twelve feet across and eighteen feet long, a platform of nearly uniform eight-inch logs laid across a rectangular frame of notched ten-inchers with a brace running from corner to corner across the middle. At the bow and at the stern we fixed a pair of upright birch poles standing a couple feet above the raft to serve as oarlocks.

As we were building our oars a scow floated by, one being rowed from bow and stern just as we intended to row ours. The big scow was difficult to bring to shore, but the two men were attempting to do just that. They called out, "Do you need help?"

Any earlier and we would have gladly accepted it. "We're okay!" we hollered back, and waved them by.

Plumb exhausted, we put back on the river twenty-three hours after we'd stopped to help the Swensons. It took both of us heaving at the sweeps, with their long angled oar blades, to keep from broaching on the heads of the islands and the gravel bars. In the brief half-light between sunset and sunrise, the Yukon finally joined together again into one broad river with the Hamlin Hills rising on both sides.

All of a sudden it came to me that in my haste to get going, I'd left the ax miles upstream—right there on the bank, where I'd last set it down. I was sick. I broke the news to Jamie. She was so exhausted, she gave it the merest shrug. "We've still got the saw."

She slept, I steered. There was no possibility of propelling the raft faster than the current. All that need be done was to steer it clear of the gravel bars. If only I could quit picturing that ax on the bank, how easy it would have been to set it on the raft. Put my brains in a jaybird's head and he'd fly backward.

Man, oh man, was I tired.

Below Rampart Canyon, a day later, the hills opened up and we were watching for a landmark that the map called Moosehead Rack.

Moosehead Rack was easy to spot. It had four distinct peaks sticking up along a ridge like tines along a moose antler. A fierce head wind had come up, and we were clinging to the right shore. A fish camp was approaching, and so was a strange mechanical device that had been placed in the river barely offshore.

It was a Ferris wheel of sorts, fifteen feet or so in diameter and powered by the current, with a wide basket of wood and metal mesh at the end of every spoke. Each basket took half its revolution underwater and the other half in the air. "It must be a fish trap of some kind," I said. "Let's go see."

We managed to beach the wallowing raft and tie up. As we were threading our way among several birchbark canoes drawn up on the shore, our eyes were drawn to a large fish thrashing in one of the baskets attached to the great wheel—a king salmon in its reddish spawning colors. The salmon was shunted from the basket into a chute and dropped into a wood box.

A boy of eight or nine walking across the gangplank from the shore to the marvelous fish trap stopped when he saw us coming his way.

"Maybe we can beg a salmon from them," Jamie whispered.

Suddenly the boy ran to the shore and disappeared.

"You grew up around Indians," I said. "What should we do?"

"Just wait. Wait right here. Someone will come out to see us."

The boy's entire family appeared, from little brothers and sisters to what might have been great-grandparents. Though we were unarmed, they seemed ill at ease.

Something was amiss. I would have thought that the sight of Burnt Paw with a bandanna tied around his neck would have made at least the small children smile.

A white-haired elder whose eyes were covered with a thin film was straining to make us out. A young woman spoke to him, describing us, I guessed.

The old man brought his right hand to his lips with a tipping motion, which he repeated several times.

"We're invited to tea," Jamie said.

SEVENTEEN

A path led onto a sunny rise overlooking the river, where the family's canvas tents were flanked by drying racks draped with surprisingly few salmon. We soon found out why.

Over tea and bannock, we learned from a girl our age who spoke English that two men had recently stopped and stolen much of their dried salmon.

We asked immediately if the two had been paddling a canoe.

"A green canoe," the girl said.

We told her that we'd had an identical canoe until they destroyed it. We also told her it was likely that the bearded one had started the fire in Dawson. She'd heard of the Great Fire.

The conversation moved rapidly, with the girl translating to her family. She seemed to be the only English speaker in camp; her name was Marie. Marie told us

129

that they were from the village of Rampart, nearby, and that she had gone to a mission school downriver.

At every fresh revelation about the men who'd robbed them, there was a great deal of chattering among the family, a great deal of outrage. The old man and a silver-haired woman who might have been his wife listened to the hubbub and sipped their tea. Their lined and leathered faces remained relatively unmoved.

Marie told us that a theft of salmon from a fish camp had never happened before, not anywhere along this piece of the river, not anywhere they knew of. This just wasn't done, stealing food. Food was always shared whenever it was requested. But these men hadn't even asked. They had simply taken.

The white-haired old man spoke for the first time.

Marie said, "He wants to know why they destroyed your canoe."

Jamie described the race, and explained that the two considered us to be their rivals.

"Ah," the old man said afterward.

"We should get back on our raft," I said to Marie as I started to rise from the log stool on which I'd been sitting. "We're hoping to overtake them."

"Their canoe is faster," Marie pointed out.

"We think they'll stop and sleep," Jamie explained. "If they do, we will quietly exchange our raft for their canoe, which used to belong to me and my father."

When Marie translated this, there was much approval all around. The old people, especially the old man, were delighted at the thought.

Then Marie whispered in Jamie's ear.

"What is it?" I asked Jamie.

"They know we're in a hurry, but they insist we share a proper meal with them."

We didn't refuse. They feasted us with delicious moose steaks and smoked salmon heaped with berries. Such an outpouring of affection I'd never seen in my life. I couldn't tell what it was, if this was the way they always were, or if they had wanted to show they didn't hold us to blame for something other white men had done.

As we were drinking tea again and sharing yet another bannock cake, the blind elder made a lengthy speech while looking at me. He seemed to be able to make out my general shape.

"Grandfather says you need to be in a canoe if you're going to race," Marie said. "A canoe is so much faster. One of our canoes."

"We couldn't bring it back," I explained.

"He'll make another one. It only takes him a few weeks. It's the right time of the year—the sap is in the birchbark and it's easy to peel."

I shook my head. "It's too great a gift."

"Grandfather says you can never catch up to them on that raft."

Jamie and I knew he was right.

The old man suddenly made another lengthy speech, which seemed to light the imagination of every man, woman, and child in the family.

Marie listened with care, then turned to us with a smile. "He says even though you are last in the race now, maybe you *can* catch up. That birchbark canoe is very light. He wants you to know that there is a portage trail from the Yukon over to the ocean. It will save you the last five hundred miles of the river."

"The shortcut!" Jamie and I exclaimed at once. "That's it! That has to be it!" Everyone watched our reaction closely. Some of the little children left off playing with Burnt Paw and clapped their hands together in excitement.

"How long is the portage?" I pressed Marie.

"Pretty long, pretty hard. He did it a long time ago, when he was young, but in the winter. It's a winter trail. The people on the Yukon use their dog teams on it when the snow and ice makes it easy. They bring back seal meat, Eskimo clothing, things like that. In the summer, Grandfather says, maybe they don't use it. Maybe it's too wet. But he remembers that the trail, after a while, follows a little river down to the village on the coast— Unalakleet. He says maybe you can carry the canoe far enough to put it on that little river, then paddle down to the ocean. Maybe you can do this. He's not sure, but he thinks so."

"Where would we find out about this trail?"

"Once the Koyukuk River comes into the Yukon, start asking."

In a few minutes' time we were repacking our gear into our two large canvas packsacks. We weeded out the iron skillet and a number of other heavy or bulky items and left them as presents.

We set to packing the birchbark canoe. It was no more than eleven feet long and a thing of beauty.

When we'd stowed the shotgun, Burnt Paw hopped inside. We took up the handsome birch paddles that came with the canoe and tried to say good-bye.

The family had turned bashful, no words at all.

"That fish trap," I said, pointing to the wheel. "What do you call it?"

"Fish wheel," Marie said. "New invention. My father and my uncle saw one last year. They made this one themselves. Pretty good, eh?"

Jamie smiled. "May all your racks be full of fish."

Marie translated what Jamie had said.

The old woman approached and placed a palm on each of our heads, and spoke a few words in her tongue.

Everyone started giggling. Marie whispered in Jamie's ear.

Jamie blushed.

With a smile for me, Jamie said, "Well, time to go, Jason."

I took my place in the bow, Jamie took hers in the stern, and Marie gave us a little push.

We paddled out until a fast piece of the current caught us, then we looked back and traded waves with them. Before long they were specks along the shore, and then the specks blinked out.

"What was that all about?" I asked Jamie. "What did the old woman say? Was it a blessing?"

"I don't think I'll tell you," Jamie said, blushing again.

"In that case, I'll throw myself in the river."

"Anything but that!" She was laughing now. "You don't want to know, Jason. Believe me, you'd be too embarrassed. I can't repeat it."

I fell to pondering what on earth this was about, but I couldn't imagine. "Please, tell me. I'm dying of curiosity."

"Are you *sure* you want to know?"

I had to think for a minute. "Yes, I'm sure."

"It was in response to me saying, 'May your racks be full of fish.' That was when the old woman put her hands on our heads. What she said was 'And may the two of you have many children.'"

"Holy smoke," I said without looking back at her.

"Holy smokes," she replied.

I closed my eyes and all I could see were those freckles on her nose. I found myself picturing that log cabin up the Koyukuk. I wanted to kiss her so badly I thought I'd explode.

EIGHTEEN

From the southeast, the large and silty Tanana River entered among sandbars and cottonwood islands. The ever-greater Yukon spread wide across a broad valley with dark spruce along the shores and hills of lighter green birch and aspen beyond. Mountain ranges in the distance hovered like clouds.

After the Tozitna came in, the Yukon split around a large island. We took the south channel. A tip from a deckhand on an upriver steamboat had us craning our necks for a mammoth. "Saw a woolly mammoth an hour ago on the south shore!" he'd called.

"Are you drunk or daft?" I'd shouted back merrily. I was punch-drunk myself from exhaustion. For two days now we hadn't slept at all. There wasn't room in the birchbark canoe, and we knew we'd lose any chance of catching up if we went to the shore to sleep.

With a hearty laugh the deckhand had called back,

"Neither. Peel your eyes for the bones of ice-age creatures down there in the mud cliffs—that stretch is called the Boneyard. Mark my words, you'll see a mammoth!"

Now our frail canoe was passing under the high mud cutbanks. Suddenly Jamie was pointing to something glinting in the light—a very large and curving piece of . . . ivory.

"Now I've seen everything," Jamie marveled.

"We have truly seen the elephant," I said, playing on the old expression for taking part in a gold rush.

Through a veil of weariness, we saw the Nowitna join the Yukon, then the Melowitna.

Some splintered lumber floating down the river caught Jamie's eye. It had large block lettering on it that looked familiar. We paddled over to see and found the letters OON from the front of the Moonlight Hotel. More likely than not, we figured, the hotel had gone down in the floodwaters.

We kept paddling. More than three hundred miles after we'd met the Swensons in the tail end of the Flats, we laid eyes on a river coming in from the north that was running clear as glass. This was the river of their dreams, the Koyukuk. Something told me this was the river of my dreams, too.

"Wouldn't you love to see that country four or five hundred miles up this Koyukuk?" I said to Jamie.

"I would," she replied. "Maybe one day we will."

Great day in the morning, but that was a mouthful.

The Koyukuk split around a large island in its mouth before its crystal waters joined the Yukon and ran side by side against the muddy torrent as far as we could see downstream. I fancied that my life and Jamie's were two rivers destined to join into one.

Or would they run separately into the sea?

At a fish camp on the island, we asked about the Swensons. The Swedes were easy to describe: man, woman, boy, girl, all with hair of gold, on a scow and hoping to catch a steamer up the Koyukuk.

"By jingo, yes," we were told by a fisherman repairing his net, and he began to elaborate. The woman behind him listened as she removed strips of salmon from the drying racks.

The fisherman had seen the Swensons the morning before in the village not far upstream. "Sorry you miss them—boat leave yesterday," he said at the end, pointing north.

"They got on the boat that went up the Koyukuk?" Jamie asked hopefully. "That would make us happy."

"By jingo, yes!"

"We're going this way," I said with a wave down the Yukon. "We're close to Nulato now, eh?"

He pointed down the Yukon. "Sure, twenty miles, no more. Right side."

"Do you know of a portage trail to the ocean?" I asked urgently.

"Twenty mile past Nulato, at little place called Kaltag. Winter trail."

"But it can be done in the summer?"

His face clouded. "Winter trail," he repeated. "Summer, pretty bad. 'Nother canoe ask me about dat portage yesterday. I say same thing."

"Was it a green canoe?" Jamie asked.

"Yeah."

They were only a day ahead, not two. We thanked the fisherman and paddled on with renewed hope and renewed trepidation.

"I'd bet Donner had only the flimsiest notion of the portage before," I said, thinking aloud. "By now he knows more, but how much? From the scale on our map, the distance of the portage from Kaltag to Unalakleet would be about eighty miles. Our map, and presumably theirs, doesn't show any rivers. When the old man gave us the birchbark canoe, he told us to paddle it down a small river. They might not know about that. If they think they would have to carry the Peterborough eighty miles overland, they won't even consider it. Maybe they'll stick with the Yukon."

Jamie looked doubtful. "They've let themselves get behind the pack. Now they have to gamble on the portage."

I said, "I have the unhappy feeling that you're right."

We clung to the right shore. It was cloudy and the wind had the ocean's salty bite to it. Our map showed we were due east of Norton Sound. The seagulls wheeling overhead might have been at the sea only hours before if they'd flown the route of the proverbial crow. Yet the Yukon was nowhere near entering the sea. From this point the great river was going to flow nearly three hundred miles south before it turned west and finally north over a course of several hundred more miles.

Whatever Donner and Brackett were going to do, *our* only chance lay in the portage.

Twenty miles down from the mouth of the Koyukuk, the cabins of Nulato came into view atop the tall riverbank. A little closer and we could make out the long green crescent of the Peterborough at the village dock. There on the bow was the red arrow Jamie had painted.

No sign of our enemies. "Here's the chance for us to return them the favor they did us," I said, my voice half strangled. "We can sink it."

"Not Father's canoe," Jamie said instantly. "We'll hide it somewhere."

"Agreed."

We were just about to come abreast of the dock. A young man came down the slanting path from the village with a fishing net in his hands and placed it in the canoe, which was otherwise empty except for a paddle.

We asked about the canoe. "They traded me for an Indian canoe like dat one you have," the young man told us with a wide smile. "Now, look, I have a Peterborough! Pretty good, eh?"

"I'm glad you have it," Jamie told him. "It used to belong to me and my father."

The young man's eyes furrowed. "Those two didn't steal it, eh?"

"My father sold it to someone else, who must have sold it to them."

"Good, that's good. You in dat race?"

"We hope we're still in it, but we're in last place."

"Hunnerts of boats come by here yesterday, last night. Those two dat traded for my canoe said they needed a lighter boat to go across to Unalakleet."

"That means they must know about a river down to the sea."

"Sure, I told 'em. I told 'em you go up the Kaltag River as far as you can go, cross over near Old Woman Mountain, then you go down Unalakleet River on the other side."

"Is it steep, the crossing between the two rivers?"

"Not steep. Swampy, lots of bugs. They tried to pay me twenty dollars to come with 'em. I just laugh. Too many bugs, an' I'm going to fish camp anyway."

"Will anyone be at Kaltag?" I asked. "In case we need more directions?"

"Maybe not. Everybody at fish camp this time of year."

"You've helped us," Jamie said. "Is there anything we can give you?"

He pointed toward Burnt Paw and chuckled. "Maybe dat big sled dog."

"You'd have to catch half the salmon in this river to feed him," I said in the same spirit. "He's got a pretty big appetite."

"Maybe not, then."

We paddled up the greenish Kaltag River accompanied by hundreds of salmon swimming in the same direction a fathom or two below. Beneath them the gray bottom was paved with the half-skeletal, half-decaying remains of their predecessors who'd washed down from upstream.

After several miles the Kaltag River resembled a creek, narrow in spots and rushing between banks covered with alders. We had to get out and walk. I pulled the canoe forward with a length of rope while Jamie nudged it around rocks and downed logs. The water poured in over the tops of our gum boots. It had been so long since our socks were dry that we took no notice.

The stench of decaying salmon was thick and oppressive. We took our time moving forward, calling out as we approached every bend so as not to surprise a bear. Their enormous tracks were everywhere in the mud. These were grizzlies. Our shotgun shells would be of no use against them. Our birdshot might not even penetrate their skin.

Burnt Paw stood at the bow of the canoe surveying the salmon. His head jerked comically from one side to the other as the big fish made furious runs upstream through the shallows. The salmon were greenish, with upright purple bars decorating their sides. They were in so little water at times that their dorsal fins sliced the air. Their violent movements and the closeness of them aroused the predator in Burnt Paw. Finally he couldn't stand it any longer—he leapt from the canoe and chased after them.

After half a dozen chases, he caught one. The fish was as long as my forearm, already disintegrating from the tail up, but full of fight. The salmon thrashed in his jaws as the mutt held it up, the motion tossing his head back and forth. Burnt Paw was proud but at a loss what to do next.

"I don't want it," I told him.

"That's a dog salmon you have there," Jamie told him. "The kind the Indians feed their dogs. Not considered the best eating by humans. It's all yours."

Exhausted by his catch or discouraged, perhaps, by Jamie's low opinion of it, Burnt Paw released the salmon on the cobbles. It was a hook-jawed male, and there appeared to be a sort of fungus growing over its fins and eyes. In all likelihood the fish was blind.

The creek was getting shallower all the time. Before long, I knew, I'd have to carry the canoe over my head.

Affected no doubt by all the dead and dying salmon, my thoughts turned gloomy. The portage might be too difficult. We might not find the river down to the sea.

"Hello, bear," Jamie kept calling. "Don't want to surprise you, bear."

Around a bend my eyes fell on two sets of gum boot tracks in the mud. "Look here," I said. "I'm afraid we know who made these."

Jamie's eyes went from the tracks to the ominously thick alders lining the route ahead. Burnt Paw perked up his ears. We listened.

All we could hear was the wind in the trees, the water rushing over the cobbles, and the buzzing of mosquitoes.

Now we really had something to be worried about.

NINETEEN

When at last we couldn't rope the canoe through the shallows any longer, we had to climb out of the creek banks and look for the portage trail.

We couldn't find one.

On both sides of the creek we found mossy bear trails with deep, alternating foot wells the size of dinner plates. Jamie and I looked at each other with eyes wide. "I've never seen the like," she said. "In the interior the bears don't get this big. The salmon must be the difference."

There was no apparent man trail. We remembered the warning that this was a winter route, and reasoned that winter passage here by sleds and dogs had left no mark on the land.

With the canoe over my head, the middle thwart biting into my shoulders and the weight of my packsack in addition, it was easy to see why neither the Indians

143

from the Yukon nor the Eskimos from the coast were fond of this route in summer.

Unable to free a hand to swat the mosquitoes swarming my face, and with the ground softening by the minute, I understood better and better.

We found our head nets, but I lacked the strength or the will to shoulder the canoe again. I looked at Jamie, saw utter exhaustion in her face. Her packsack was heavier than mine; I could see her staring at it on the ground. The limit to her endurance was bound to be close if I'd nearly reached mine.

"I'm done in," I said.

"We've gone far enough," she agreed. "The sun will set in an hour. I can't even remember when we slept last. We can only do so much."

We backed into the spruce forest where the mosquitoes were fewer and built a smoky fire to keep them at bay. We brewed tea and we ate dried salmon and bannock cakes. With our strength revived a little, we took the saw, made poles, and erected the tent. We draped our big piece of netting over the entire tent. As we got into our bedrolls I mumbled a worry about our dried salmon and the bears. With a yawn Jamie said, "The bears have plenty of fresh salmon; they won't care for dried."

"I'm happy to hear that," I said.

We were facing each other, and our lips were only inches apart. Her eyes were closed. I touched my lips to hers. After a moment, she kissed me back, lightly. I freed a hand and stroked her hair. She opened her eyes and found mine.

"Dawson City seems so far away, Jason."

"I know. We're a whole lot closer to Nome than Dawson. But honestly, today I had my doubts."

She put her hand to my cheek. "I have a feeling it's

going to get harder. But we can't give up. We've come too far."

"You're still undaunted."

"I've been thinking about the women I met climbing the Chilkoot Pass with loads on their backs. Even when it was straight up at the last and too difficult to be believed, I never saw one give up."

"Me neither, and I spent a lot of time on the Chilkoot."

"All the same, I feel like I've been beat with a stick over every inch of my body. Jason, we have to reduce the weight. What can we get rid of?"

"Any number of things, I hope. Wait a minute, I'm still carrying Dr. Kilmer's Swamp Root."

"You actually have that? What is it?"

"A liquid, I can tell you that much. A fellow back in Dawson threw it into my outfit for free."

"Don't dump it in a stream. It might kill all the salmon."

Chuckling at the thought, I whispered, "I'm drawing strength from you, Jamie."

"And I from you. Keep remembering about getting the mill back, Jason. No matter what, we can't let that murderer get his hands on our twenty thousand dollars."

"Twenty thousand dollars," I whispered, and then I slept like the dead.

We woke to birds squawking and Burnt Paw growling. A pair of ravens had landed on our packsacks and were tearing at the heavy canvas with their powerful black beaks. Burnt Paw surprised one of them with a coiled leap and came back to earth with tail feathers in his mouth. The ravens flew to a nearby tree and squawked what I presumed to be profanities at him until we were under way again. The sun was far above the horizon. By Jamie's watch it was seven in the morning.

Ten miles off, perhaps, a lone mountain rose in the distance. Old Woman Mountain, we figured. By a stretch of the imagination we could even make out head and feet.

The tracks of our enemies in the soft ground began to aim to the right, to pass the mountain on the north.

Having no desire to run into them, we aimed to the left, to clear the mountain on the south.

Jamie walked in front with the heavy packsack, the shotgun tied on the back with slipknots.

The bow of the canoe blocked my view. Mostly I kept my eyes on the ground, careful to choose the best footing to support the weight I was carrying. I had a close view of the fine spruce-root cordage that fastened the gunwales, and my nostrils were full of the scent of spruce pitch from all the caulking that waterproofed the canoe. I tried to think about how light this canoe was compared to the Peterborough. Birchbark, thin slats of birchwood, rootlets, pitch, that's all it was.

That's all.

Why did it bite so fiercely into my shoulders, and why did the back of my neck feel as if it had been gored by a bull?

The divide that separated the Yukon from the Bering Sea was not a high one, thank God, with the exception of Old Woman Mountain, which we were skirting. The climbing was steady but never steep, through birch and aspen thickets and underneath the dark spruce forest. Our constant companions were ravens and gray jays. Burnt Paw chased red squirrels and nearly got himself a noseful of porcupine quills before I managed to call him back, just in time. Game trails were everywhere, with sign of moose and smaller droppings we guessed were left by caribou.

In the forest we could no longer see Old Woman Mountain. I couldn't tell west from east. Jamie had grown up nearly at this latitude and seemed to have a sense of direction from the position of the circling sun and the time of day. I was hopeful that our enemies were thoroughly lost.

When at last we crested the hills, the vast land spreading before us and to both sides took us by surprise. It was treeless. We were looking at an immense expanse of tundra barrens dotted with ponds and lakes but lacking anything like a river canyon.

Carefully, I lowered the canoe to one knee, then to the ground. "Where, in all that, might the Unalakleet River be hiding?"

Jamie shook her head. "If we can't find it, it's going to be a long walk to the sea."

We made our way down out of the hills and onto the barrens, where the spongy mosses and white lichens gave with every step. We had to skirt the muskeg swamps, and the ponds grew in size and number. The mosquitoes were a maddening, droning horde and would have made short work of our sanity if not for the netting and our gloves. Midday, the wind came up in advance of ribbed clouds speeding inland and kept the mosquitoes at bay.

We kept slogging, endlessly. At last the sky was a riot of reds and oranges. The sun was close to setting. I put the canoe down and threw myself next to it on my back.

We hadn't found a river.

I doubted I could continue. Jamie must have felt the same. "My suggestion is," she said wearily, "we give up for today and sleep."

There were bushes nearby with scraps of dead wood, but we were too exhausted to make a fire, even a small one for tea. There were no poles for pitching our tent. We sank the blades of our canoe paddles in the tundra and draped the tent over them as best we could.

As we were about to crawl under the canvas we heard a gunshot, and then a second.

We strained to see where the blasts had come from. We made out, across the undulations of the tundra, a mother bear and two small cubs running in our general direction, in all likelihood from the gunfire. They seemed to be fleeing an unnatural feature beyond them, a tiny patch of white—a tarp or tent. Now we made out the figures of two men over there.

"No doubt it's Donner and Brackett," I whispered. "Let's keep down. Maybe they won't notice us way over here."

"Are the bears still coming our way?"

"They're down in a swale. They could've turned another direction. No way to tell which way they're moving."

Burnt Paw hadn't seen the threat, but the gunshots and the tone of our voices had him sheltering right between us where we lay.

Bears move fast. It took little time to find out they'd kept running in our direction. A short while later, bounding out of the swale, here they came. They were startled to suddenly find us in front of them. All three of them, the mother and her little cubs, stood on hind legs and inspected us from no more than fifty feet.

I knew black bears, and these weren't black bears. They were brown bears, wide-faced, with humps on their backs and long claws on their front feet. Grizzlies.

The cubs wheeled away to the side, but their mother didn't. She woofed a couple of times, clacked her teeth, laid back her ears, then came charging right for us. We were still on our bellies, and I reached instinctively for the shotgun an arm's length away. I came to my senses and let it be.

No more than ten feet away, the mother grizzly rose to her full height and let out a horrible roar. The stench from her gut washed over us. One moment I felt Burnt Paw's trembling body at my side, the next he let out a yelp and ran the opposite way.

The grizzly swayed on her hind feet, watching Burnt Paw go, watching us. Now that she could see exactly what we were, she wheeled in the direction of her cubs.

As soon as the grizzly had her cubs at her side, she stood up for another look at us, the cubs doing the same; then she woofed and laid her ears back again.

"Oh, no," I heard Jamie whisper, as here came the grizzly, charging fast and furious as before. Jamie's hand found mine and we held on tight.

As before, the grizzly pulled up short, stood, roared, and roared again.

Once again, it proved only a warning. She went to all fours, retreated slightly, glanced once over her shoulder at us, then bounded back to her cubs. This time she collected them and was gone.

"I just died of fright," Jamie told me.

"You're not the only one. Where's Burnt Paw?"

"He'll come back. Poor fellow—he was so scared."

An hour later Burnt Paw wasn't back, and an hour after that, with the sun rising again, he still hadn't returned. "Maybe we should just go to sleep," Jamie suggested. "He'll come back."

"If he's lost, should we take the time to search for him?"

"You should decide that."

I thought hard. "I can't leave him," I said finally. "Darned dog."

I got in my bag. Before long I heard Jamie's breathing start to come with a little whistle. I was about to let myself fall into exhaustion's tomb as well, when my thoughts turned to Donner and Brackett. My breathing came fast; I was filled with dread. Without doubt they'd seen our tent. They'd know it was us. What would they do if they caught us unawares?

They wouldn't come after us, I realized, they'd come after the canoe—just like before. With birchbark it would take so little.

I slipped out of my bedroll. Keeping low to the ground, I took the shotgun with me and hid behind the scrub willows at a spot that gave me a line of sight at the approach to our camp and our canoe.

I waited.

TWENTY

It wasn't an hour before a bit of motion between the scrub willows caught my eye. It was Donner, keeping low with an ax in one hand, a rifle in the other.

I held my position and let him keep coming. Donner halted behind the last piece of scrub between him and the canoe, then peeked around the side of the willows at the canoe and the tent.

Put the rifle down, I thought. To bash the canoe in, you need both hands on the ax.

Donner put the rifle down on the ground, and then he put the ax down. Eyes constantly on the tent door, he touched his hand to the hilt of the sheath knife at his side.

Donner started out across the clearing empty-handed, but now his hand was going to the knife again. I understood clear as day. He'd seen we had a birchbark canoe, not the Peterborough. The knife would be quieter.

"Don't," I said in a low voice.

Donner swiveled toward me as I rose to my knees, keeping the barrel aimed at his heart. His face was a sunburned mask of surprise, all welted above his beard from mosquito bites. He'd lost his hat and lacked mosquito netting, and I didn't feel a bit sorry for him.

"Touch that knife and I'll blow you to kingdom come," I told him.

He must have thought I meant it. I wasn't sure if I did or not. I only knew he might be able to throw that knife.

Donner broke into a broad smile. "Hawthorn, it's you!"

"Indeed it is."

"Why are you whispering?"

He was using his phony voice on me, the soothing one. Watch it, I told myself. This is a murderer.

"I aim to let Jamie sleep. She needs it. What are you doing here, Donner?"

"Come to see if our neighbors were okay, of course. Put the shotgun down, Hawthorn, there's no call for it."

"Why did you bring a rifle and an ax?"

"It's bear country, or haven't you noticed? I came over to see if whoever was here was okay. We scared some grizzlies away from our camp. They ran this direction. You must have seen them."

"Oh, we saw them. Have you seen my dog?"

"Scared off, was he? That's too bad. We'll sure keep our eyes open. For God's sake put the shotgun aside, Hawthorn. What's eating you?"

"Don't you remember our Peterborough?"

"Of course—it was just like ours. I suppose you've traded it for a lighter one, same as us. What of it?"

"You felled a tree on it back in the Flats."

Donner feigned surprise. "Surely you don't think me capable of such an act."

"Oh, I do. Not only that, I think you came over here to find out if your neighbors—whoever they might be—had a canoe. From what happened to us back in the Flats, I'd say you take this race far too seriously."

He snorted. "We'll complete it, for sport, but we've lost our chance of winning. We've been wandering around lost the last two days with no idea where to put our canoe in the water. The natives give such flimsy directions."

"I know."

"Hawthorn, we're both in the same predicament. We should team up, at least until we reach the sea."

"You'll help us find my dog, then? Because we aren't going anywhere until we find him."

Donner laughed. "You'd give up the chance at twenty thousand dollars to search for that miserable excuse for a canine? I remember him as quite unpleasant."

"He's the better judge of character."

"You're as unpleasant as him! Now, put the shotgun down. You wouldn't use it anyway, I know you wouldn't."

"You've checked on your 'neighbors'—we're fine, thank you. Now you can go back to your camp. I hope you're remembering your promise to sell me the mill. . . ."

His sly smile was back on his face. "For twenty thousand dollars, as I recall."

"In a turkey dream. That's too high."

Donner shrugged. "I'll find another buyer."

I motioned with the shotgun for him to leave. "Goodbye, Donner."

"We'll see you in Nome, then, if not before. Meanwhile, good luck on finding a river."

"Same to you. All the luck in the world."

"Get some rest, now. . . ."

Donner retrieved his ax and rifle without looking back. I watched him disappear into the folds of the tundra. At last I could put the shotgun down.

Jamie poked her head out of the tent. "You saved the canoe, Jason—thank goodness for that. I was listening carefully. Donner still can't tell if we know about the detective and the fire and all that. He thinks you had the shotgun on him because of what he did to us back in the Flats."

"That's what I was hoping."

"If I'm wrong, he'll try to murder us both."

I crawled back into the tent. "Now, that's encouraging."

"They'll find the river. They'll be on their way."

"Why do you say that?"

"Just a hunch. Those bears must have come down out of the hills to feed on the salmon. That's what the bears are doing this time of year. We must be close to a river."

By the time we woke, no vestige of Donner and Brackett could be seen across the way, and Burnt Paw still wasn't back. Calling at the top of our lungs, we started out in the direction he'd run. As we were about to lose sight of camp, I had Jamie stand still and I made my way out across the spongy terrain, in and out of hollows but never losing sight of her. All the while I kept calling.

At the extremity of sight distance from Jamie—a mile or more—I saw a moving patchwork climbing out of a steep draw: a herd of caribou. The ones at the back were shaking themselves out as if they'd just been swimming.

"Burnt Paw!" I hollered into the emptiness. "Burnt Paw! Burnt Paw!"

That shrill bark of his was faint at first, but unmistakable. I yelled with all my might, and at last he came running, a tiny speck in the vastness.

That dog was so happy he ran circles around me, leapt in the air like a jack-in-the-box, nearly licked me to death. I fell to the tundra and grabbed him to my chest.

On our return he jumped into Jamie's arms and went just as crazy over her. "Look who's back!" she exclaimed.

"I may have found the river," I reported.

Indeed I had. It was more of a creek, but it was deep enough to float the canoe and, even more importantly, was teeming with salmon. It would lead us to the sea.

It was with the greatest relief, several hours later, that we floated the canoe and started paddling downstream. It would be too soon if I never walked another step on tundra.

As it turned out, Donner and Brackett had found another fork of the same stream. Where the two joined, we saw them paddling down the other fork. They slipped in a few hundred yards behind us.

Frequent creeks added volume to the river. With our enemies at our backs, we paddled over salmon and among waterfowl taking explosively to the air.

The river was never fast, never rocky. The sea, we guessed, was no more than sixty miles away.

We flew. We were anxious that Donner and Brackett not overtake us, for fear they would wait in ambush around a bend.

For whatever reason, they seemed content with the distance between the canoes. By the time the sun set, we could no longer see them behind. We wondered if they had stopped to sleep.

"Shall we keep pushing?" I asked. "All the way to Unalakleet?"

"To U-na-la-kleet," Jamie chanted, "counting no sheep."

"To U-na-la-fad-dle," I chanted back, "flashing our paddles."

"To U-na-la-muck," she sang, "dodging the ducks."

"To U-na-la-dish," I sang, "bumping the fish."

We kept on this way until we ran out of rhymes.

The sun rose and resumed its great circle around the sky. We kept paddling. At three in the afternoon, with the gulls crying and wheeling overhead, and the ocean air palpable in a thick mist, we spied the white spire of a church atop the headlands, and then a settlement of huts fashioned from bleached driftwood and whalebone.

Unalakleet.

TWENTY–ONE

Atop a long spit, the village momentarily passed from view as we paddled under the headlands. We could plainly hear the surf ahead.

Where the river shallowed and spilled through the beach, we stepped out of the canoe and stood up gingerly, easing our aching backs.

We were looking at the Bering Sea, gray as the clouds overhead.

A Yukon sternwheeler, the *Bonanza King*, was anchored offshore. Skin boats with half a dozen paddlers were lightering supplies from the vessel to the beach. Hundreds of men, women, and children were spilling down from the village atop the spit angling into the sea.

We withdrew our canoe from the water and carried it up the beach where the tide couldn't reach it. Except by the round-faced children who stared, we were generally ignored. We went to see what we could learn.

Numbers of Eskimos loosely surrounded three white men on the beach. From the fringes of the crowd we ascertained that the one who'd come ashore with the supplies was a representative of the Alaska Commercial Company. The brisk weather, or else his impatience, had flushed his face a bright red. His counterpart from the trading post in Unalakleet was alternately adding figures and tugging on his walrus mustache. The third, in a black robe, was an old priest with a beard as white as the caribou moss on the tundra. The priest stood to the side, silent.

The visiting trader was in a hurry to return to the sternwheeler. "There are four hundred and fifty-three stampeders on the *Bonanza King* desperate to stake claims at Cape Nome," I heard him say. "If I delay them, they'll lynch me."

We nudged our way closer. If he was about to leave, I knew I'd better speak up. At his elbows, I asked, "What news of the Great Race?"

The three noticed us for the first time and stared dumbfounded. "Who are you and where in the world did you come from?" asked the red-faced trader from the sternwheeler.

"Jason Hawthorn and Jamie Dunavant," I answered. "We've just come down the Unalakleet River. We're registered in the race."

There was a sudden commotion in the crowd, which parted as two men, bug-bitten and sunburned, came pushing their way through—Donner and Brackett. "Who are you?" Donner demanded of the traders as he panted for breath. Donner had noticed us, of course, but was acting as if we weren't there.

With raised eyebrow, the trader from the ship replied

stiffly, "My name is Hurley, of the Alaska Commercial Company. These gentlemen are George Thompson, from the A.C.C. post in Unalakleet, and Father Karloff, from the Russian church here. And you are . . . ?"

Donner hesitated, and I knew why. The bloodhound who was after him was neither of these two, but he might be close. If Donner gave his name, it would be dangerous for him. But if he didn't, he couldn't win. If he intended to win, he had to stick with the name under which he'd registered.

"Donner and Brackett," he replied, a note of desperation in his not-so-smooth voice. "We're in the race."

Hurley nodded. There was no indication in his eyes that he'd been alerted to these names.

The detective might be on his way down the Yukon, I realized, but he hadn't overtaken the *Bonanza King*.

Should I denounce Donner here and now for a criminal?

I knew I couldn't. They wouldn't hold him, not without evidence.

Hurley glanced at Brackett. The boxer looked quickly away. In all likelihood he was under orders not to speak.

"Now, what about the race?" Donner demanded. "How stands the race?"

"I'm in a hurry," Hurley said. "This much I can tell you. We reached the mouth of the Yukon at Kutlik by the northern channel ahead of every boat in the race."

"Did you talk to them?" Donner interrupted. "Those at the head of the race? What were their intentions when they reached the sea? Attempt a direct crossing of Norton Sound to Cape Nome? Hug the shore to St. Michael before crossing? Follow the shore all the way around without attempting a crossing at all?"

"What do you think?" Hurley asked Thompson. "Do the rules allow me to reply?"

The trader from Unalakleet tucked his pencil behind his ear. "The rules are posted, and they're precious few."

"I'll tell you, then. Weather allowing, they plan a direct crossing of the sound, with Eskimo guides leading the way. That seems to be the common strategy. To skirt the coast all the way to Nome would add a hundred miles or more. Some plan to use their skiffs, others to paddle native craft."

"And where do you reckon the leaders are at this moment?"

Hurley thought about it. "Just reaching the sea, same as you."

"That's what we needed to know!" Donner cried jubilantly. To Thompson, he said, "We'll need some supplies from your store, and for you to recommend a craft for us and to arrange for the sale of it."

"In good time," Thompson replied, and returned to adding a column of figures.

Hurley's eyes went from Donner and Brackett to Jamie and me. "We'll tell Nome about you, both teams. Two teams having made the portage will add a great deal of interest. Nome knows all about the race. Every man on the beach will be on the lookout and will know your names."

For the briefest moment Donner's flint-hard eyes seemed to me to flicker with fear. Then he caught himself. "Will the money be ready, in cash, for the victors?"

With a grin, Hurley replied, "Aye, it's ready."

Donner hesitated, then asked in perfect command of himself, "What are our chances of catching a big steamer heading south? Quickly, that is. If we win, we have no use for Nome."

"Steamers come and go every day, that's what I've been hearing."

"Good," Donner said. "That's good."

Within minutes Hurley was being paddled back out to the *Bonanza King*. Donner and Brackett were following Thompson up the path to the trading post.

The old priest saw us standing there, at an utter loss, watching them go. He motioned after Thompson and our enemies. "Why you two not go with?"

"We have no money," Jamie replied.

"Ah . . . ," he said ponderously. "Always a problem."

I'd been studying the skin boats drawn up on the beach. How were Donner and Brackett going to control a boat that large, even if it was light? "Those boats over there," I said. "Can two people handle those?"

The priest shook his head. "Those are for hunting whales. Seven paddles, harpooner. You need two-man kayak. All covered with skin, even the top. For hunting seals and sea lions."

"That's what we need," Jamie said.

"Lots of work to make one. Eskimos don't giff 'em away. Anyway, you can't cross without Eskimo guides. Out on the ocean, no land in sight, the Eskimos always know where they are. Birds, sun, current, wind . . . I been in this land before it was sold to the Americans, and I could not paddle to Cape Nome if my life depend on it."

"Those other two men are going to hire guides," I said. "We could follow along."

"What an idea!" Jamie encouraged me.

"All we need is a kayak," I begged.

The priest rolled his eyes.

"We have paddles," I said, just to keep talking. "Maybe we can trade our birchbark canoe for one of those kayaks you mentioned."

The priest heaved a sigh. "Those Indian canoes are worthless on the ocean. Paddles worthless, too. For kayak you need blades on both ends—paddle both sides, quick, quick. I wish I could help you."

The old Russian bent to pet Burnt Paw, who as usual was favoring his right front foot. "Got a thorn, little one? Let me see if I can help you."

"He burned his paw in a fire," I explained.

"Ah," the priest said sympathetically, "hurt your foot."

Suddenly the old man's eyes lit like bright candles. "Wait a minute. That gives me idea."

"Tell us," Jamie urged.

"Haff my life, I try to build hospital here. No money! Always, no money. That prize for winning this race, it's twenty tousand dollars, eh?"

Jamie and I nodded vigorously.

"You two, me, makes three. I find you kayak, I become equal partner. You win, I get almost seven tousand dollars for hospital."

I hesitated. I glanced at Jamie. Without a word spoken, we agreed.

"It's for a good cause," Jamie said. With a chuckle, she added, "God would be on our side, Jason."

The old priest laughed. "You bet your britches."

"It's a deal," I told him. "Now, let's hurry!"

TWENTY-TWO

In less than an hour's time we had our kayak. It was slim as a needle at the bow and stern and no wider than thirty inches across its midpoint. Its frame was made of whittled driftwood, and its sheath, tight as drum, was fashioned from sealskins. The cordage was fashioned from their sinews. Openings fore and aft allowed entry; skirts made of seal gut would cinch around our waists and keep out the sea.

By this time, six Eskimos were launching one of their skin whaleboats. With a wild cry they paddled through the light surf. To our chagrin, Donner and Brackett launched a kayak right behind them.

"We better start," I fretted, "or we'll lose them."

"Everyone out there has gut jackets and pants," the old priest said. "Waterproof. You need those. Wait a minute—I sent for them."

Jamie said, "I understand why those two are in such

163

a hurry, but why the Eskimos?"

"Same reason as riverboat. The weather is good, but it could change. They have a far way to go."

"How long will the crossing take?"

The priest shrugged. "No wind, about twenty-six hours."

An Eskimo girl came running down from the village with our jackets and pants in hand. Daylight shone through them, yet they were obviously sturdy. We put them on. They had drawstrings at the hood, wrists, and waist. They weighed almost nothing.

We stowed the small sacks of food that Father Karloff had provided for us, our flasks of water, and a few bare essentials from our previous outfit. If we were to have a chance, we had to go light.

It was 5:30 P.M. by Jamie's watch when we floated the kayak. My bladder was as empty as I could possibly manage. This was going to be a test of more than one kind of endurance.

I stepped gingerly into the bow and Jamie took her place in the stern. Sure he was being left behind, Burnt Paw was whimpering in the arms of the priest. To the mutt's great relief the priest waded out and handed him to me. I placed him on my lap, then cinched the kayak skirt loosely at my waist to allow him room to see and breathe.

With a glance over my shoulder at Jamie, I caught her unprepared as she was struggling to find a comfortable position in her low-slung seat. Her eyes were bloodshot and she looked positively gaunt, on the verge of collapse.

At that moment, all the excitement went out of me. I was filled with foreboding and dread. The Yukon River had been almost like a friend. We knew nothing of the cruel, dark face of the sea.

"What is it, Jason?"

With a rueful laugh, I said, "I'm not sure, of a sudden. I want us to live through this."

For nearly half a minute Jamie closed her eyes and said nothing. When she opened them, she said, "We won't be alone. If we get into trouble, the Eskimos will fish us into their boat. I'll always wonder if we could have won, and so will you."

Her face was still drawn, but her hazel eyes were revived and flashing fire.

She'd revived me, too. In every bone and muscle I could feel how badly I wanted to get to Nome and get there first. "Let's catch them, then, before they're out of sight!"

We paddled head-on toward the surf. The double-bladed paddles propelled the light, streamlined craft remarkably quickly. The kayak cleaved the waves like a knife blade, and we cleared the surf in a wild spray of splash and foam. Ahead, the rolling gray sea.

"Godspeed," called the old priest. "Don't forget my hospital!"

It was difficult to make out the kayak ahead and the whaleboat in front of it. All of us were paddling directly into the sun, low over the sea to the northwest.

"No worries," Jamie called confidently from the stern. "We'll catch them."

"No worries," I repeated.

We caught up hours later, as the sun was setting. We approached no closer to the kayak than a hundred yards.

It was some time before Brackett, in the stern, happened to glance back over his shoulder.

A second or two later, Donner glanced over his.

"Bet they're surprised," I said.

An hour later the sun came back up.

We paddled briskly at the very margin of endurance. Hour after hour, the pace never slackened.

By now we couldn't see land in any direction.

When the sun was high, the wind picked up. It started to drive swells at us, hills that had to be climbed.

On the uphill we had to paddle hard lest we lose momentum and be tipped sideways. Handled properly, the kayak was remarkably stable, but sideways we'd be flipped in an instant.

We paddled on. The wind pushed the swells to greater heights. We dreaded storm clouds on the horizon but saw only a thin veil of vapor high, high above.

Many hours later, when the sun was at its highest, Donner suddenly hollered to the whaleboat ahead. The Eskimos stopped paddling. As the kayak pulled alongside the whaleboat, we remained behind.

The Eskimos were all looking at us.

"What's going on?" I asked.

"I don't know," Jamie said hoarsely. She opened her spray cover and took out her flask of water. "What are they doing up there?"

The Eskimos were working to secure a length of rope from the stern of the whaleboat to the bow of the kayak. I couldn't believe my eyes.

Seconds later, paddles were flashing and they were under way again. Unwilling to believe what we were seeing, we wallowed in the swells. The Eskimos had the kayak under tow.

"Donner and Brackett wore out," Jamie called. "From battling the wind."

"It's no wonder."

"I'm racking my memory to recall the rules."

"Me too. I'm afraid it said you can't get an assist from a *motor* craft."

"You're right. The rules said nothing about an assist from a man-powered craft. Hard to admit, but I suppose they aren't breaking the rules."

"Surely the judges would disqualify them. How could it be anything but cheating?"

"I don't know. Maybe the Alaska Commercial Company won't be able to do anything about it."

We started after them, but it didn't take long to discover that we couldn't keep up.

"They're pulling away," I said with undisguised panic.

"We have to keep up," Jamie called breathlessly.

We both started paddling hard, just as hard as we could. It didn't need to be said what our chances were if we were left behind on this sea, far, far from the sight of land.

For several hours or more, we battled to keep them in sight. The swells had died down and the face of the sea was calm once again, but no matter how hard we gasped for breath, no matter how hard we paddled, the boats ahead in the hard glare of the sun kept slipping into the distance.

Finally, on the very horizon, they blinked out.

"Stop," called Jamie. "Stop paddling, Jason. I can't see them anymore."

"I know. I know."

For a long time we said nothing, just wallowed in the swells. Burnt Paw rolled his eyes up at me.

"What should we do, Jamie?"

She opened the kayak skirt, then the drawstring at her waist, and fished her father's gold watch from her pocket. "It's three-thirty in the afternoon. We've been under way for twenty-three hours."

"Do you think we're close to Nome?"

"The wind slowed us down so much, I don't think so. Not at all."

"We can tell direction by the sun, can't we?"

"Only vaguely. For a couple hours tonight, we'll have the North Star. By the map, Nome is north-by-northwest of Unalakleet. We could keep the North Star almost completely to our right. . . ."

"But that would help for only a few hours."

"We're lost, Jason. When the wind comes up again we can paddle with it and assume it will push us to land. That's all I can think of."

"You sound almost calm."

"That's because I'm terrified."

"Thank you for saying so. I was afraid it was only me."

I reached my hand back and she clasped it.

I said, "You could've been on the stage today, in some big city."

"I don't have any regrets," she said softly. "I'm like you. Whatever happens, I have to live life on my own hook—even if there's only hours left of it," she added with a desperate laugh. "I'm starving, Jason, what about you? If I'm to be lost at sea, I'd rather have something in my stomach."

We found the waterproof sacks that the priest had provided and discovered hard biscuits, dried fruit, dried salmon. We ate ravenously.

I fed bits of salmon to Burnt Paw. "Burnt Paw isn't worried," I said.

"Look!" Jamie cried. "A boat!"

She was pointing to the right of our bow. In the distance I saw the prow of a boat and the flash of paddles.

"Coming this way!" I exclaimed. "What's going on?

Is it that same whaleboat, or another?"

It was the same one. After several more minutes we could make out a kayak behind the whaleboat and slightly to the side. Both boats were coming our direction. Before long we could discern that the kayak was no longer under tow.

We finished our meal as we watched the slow approach of the boats. Several hundred yards away, just as we could begin to distinguish their faces, the Eskimos stopped paddling, the kayak as well.

The Eskimos waved us toward them.

We put away our provisions and began to paddle.

As soon as we did so, the whaleboat wheeled about and paddled away again.

"I think I understand," I said. "When the Eskimos looked back and saw that we weren't even in sight, they came back for us."

"I bet anything Donner ordered them not to, but they wouldn't obey."

"And our friends lost their tow. The Eskimos must have taken a dim view of attempted murder."

"All of a sudden I feel stronger. Let's catch up, eh? We're back in the race!"

Within half an hour we'd caught them. After that we stayed a slim fifty yards behind Donner and Brackett. The sun was sinking fast now, and we were paddling directly into it.

It set in a red blaze of glory. With the glare gone, the twilight revealed the silhouettes of great ships ahead, half a dozen of them, and beyond, a thin line along the horizon.

"Ships!" I cried. "Land! Nome!"

"Now look over your left shoulder, Jason. Tell me what you see."

"A Yukon river paddle wheeler! Hundreds of people at the rails! Stampeders from Dawson!"

"Look what's around it."

"Boats! Skiffs!"

"A dozen or more, coming hard. They're racing, and the people on the sternwheeler are watching. Do you think they see us?"

"No doubt. Now comes the real race, Jamie—let's show 'em some smoke. Let's paddle like there's no tomorrow."

TWENTY-THREE

As three quick blasts came from the sternwheeler's steam whistle, I stole a quick backward glance over my left shoulder. With much chuffing and belching of smoke, the steamboat left the skiffs behind.

I returned my attention to Donner and Brackett. Stroke by stroke, we were gaining on them. Jamie veered us slightly left, to give us room to pass them.

As we came abreast of them the sternwheeler appeared on our left, no more than a hundred yards away and slightly behind. It was the *Eldorado*, and its captain was being careful not to raise a wake that might affect the race. From the corner of my eye I saw hundreds of people crowding the rails, raising their hats and waving. Over the racket of the steam engine and three more whistle blasts I could hear the shouts and the cheers. Burnt Paw was in a frenzy on my lap, barking to the left at the sternwheeler and to the right at our enemies.

The Eskimos had fallen in behind the two kayaks in order to watch us race, and were chanting, "Ai-ee! Ai-ee! Ai-ee!"

From the shore, perhaps in response to the stern-wheeler's whistle, perhaps because people had been watching with telescopes, a fleet of small boats rowed out to meet us. They made a wide path for our kayak and its twin, tied neck and neck for the lead.

The sun was just starting to rise. It must have been one in the morning.

We passed among the giant ocean steamers anchored a mile or so from shore. I was aware of them towering above us, but I never took the time to look.

With a quick glance to my right I saw the muscles in Donner's neck corded to bursting. I remembered him whipping me when we arm-wrestled. Brackett's height came to mind, how much leverage it gave him.

Merely thinking about their advantages sapped me of what strength I had left—there was suddenly little power in my stroke. Donner and Brackett started to slip ahead.

"Paddle!" Jamie cried. "Paddle for the mill, Jason! Paddle as you love me!"

I forgot about Donner. I forgot about Brackett. I barely noticed all the people waving from small boats along our route. Their shouts seemed to come from a great distance. I put my mind on my brothers, on the mill, on Jamie, on my paddle.

Finally I could see, at the mouth of a tundra river, a tent metropolis with a sprinkling of buildings beyond. Nome.

Pull! I told myself. Pull, pull!

I kept the double-bladed paddle moving with everything I had, not too deep, not too shallow. Let Jamie make the steering adjustments, I told myself, you just give it the power. Give it more power.

More power!

I could see the crowd at the landing now. I could hear a tumultuous roar. There must be thousands, I thought. Thousands.

Pull! Remember how that husky of yours could pull. King, for the love of heaven, help me!

Remember what your brother suffered to stay in the ring with the Sydney Mauler. To beat him!

I kept pulling with all I had.

No matter how hard we tried, we couldn't seem to gain on them. But they weren't putting any distance on us—they were barely ahead.

The crowd at the beach was parting to make a lane.

"Remember, the Alaska Commercial Company building!" Jamie cried. "We'll have to run for it!"

A hundred yards to the beach. Everybody waving their hats. A sea of arms and hats and blurred faces.

The lane. Keep your eye on the lane. Straight as an arrow to the lane.

Keep paddling!

The two kayaks were no more than ten feet apart. Over the roar of the crowd I could hear Donner wheezing for breath. I caught a glimpse of Brackett's granite face turned beet red.

At the last, the beach and crowd seemed to surge forward. Suddenly we were scraping bottom.

"Let's go!" came Jamie's cry.

I was fumbling with the drawstring of the kayak skirt. It wouldn't come loose. I ripped it loose, tried to lift myself out of the kayak, fell sideways into the water and almost onto Burnt Paw. Jamie was staggering beside me, trying to give me a hand up.

Donner had tripped, too, face forward on the beach. Brackett yanked him up; the four of us stumbled forward like drunks. After so long in the kayaks, it was impossible to walk, much less run.

On both sides voices were shouting that we had to touch the Alaska Commercial Company building. A man wearing a derby hat was shouting, "I'm from the A.C.C. Follow me, I'll run straight to it!"

Jamie and I held hands to try to keep each other up, ran and stumbled and staggered forward.

A yelp, and Jamie went down.

The yelp was from Burnt Paw. He'd gotten under her feet.

I gave Jamie two hands and pulled her up. We were looking at Donner's and Brackett's backs.

The boxer ran ahead. We had a chance of catching Donner. I could hear his wheezing.

Burnt Paw ran out in front of us, looking behind over his shoulder, looking to his side at Donner.

In the midst of my delirium I noticed one of his ears was up, one down.

There, written large across the second story of a building in the next block, was the lettering ALASKA COMMERCIAL COMPANY.

Feeling had fully returned to our legs, and we were running as fast as we could run.

But we weren't going to catch Brackett.

Maybe not Donner, either.

"Burnt Paw!" I warned. Zigzagging, he was about to run under my feet.

Barely in time, the mutt looked over his shoulder and saw me, accelerated, and veered off to the right, in front of Donner.

The roar from the throng was deafening. Brackett

had touched the building. Forty feet to go and Donner had two steps on us.

Burnt Paw looked over his shoulder at Donner, but too late.

With his last spurt of energy, Donner was upon him.

I saw Burnt Paw try to get out of the way. He veered left, but so did Donner. Cornelius Donner went down in a heap, and we ran past him.

Jamie and I touched the corner of the building together. The man with the derby hat lifted her arm and mine in triumph.

"The winners!" he proclaimed, tossing his derby in the air. "Both must finish, and these just did!"

Jamie and I collapsed against the building.

I embraced her, let her go. Heaving for breath, I slumped against the building. Neither of us could speak. Tears popped from Jamie's eyes, then mine gushed. Burnt Paw came between us, licked us both on the face.

Donner was above us crying foul. "Their dog tripped me! You saw it plainly!"

"Tripped her, too," the official from the A.C.C. said dryly. "Anyway, there's nothing in the rules about being tripped by dogs."

A laugh went up from the crowd. The throng was so close, I was suffocating.

"Stand back! Stand back. Give them room. What are your names as registered?"

"Hawthorn and Dunavant," I gasped.

"Check the list!"

The official was handed a sheaf of papers, flipped through them, and fingered his way down a page. "Here they are! Jason Hawthorn and Jamie Dunavant."

"That's us," Jamie said.

We struggled to our feet as the cheers kept coming,

along with hearty slaps on the back. All of a sudden I
thought how strange we must look in our gut pants and
jackets.

"Stand back, stand back!"

At last, room to breathe. Just then a grizzled fellow
stepped out of the crowd, walked up close to Jamie, and
looked at her oddly. He inspected her from several
angles, then stepped back into the crowd, said something to a second graybeard, who stepped forward and
did the same thing—looked at Jamie this way and that.
A smile broke out on his face like he'd just discovered a
vein of solid gold.

"What is it?" demanded the official. "What is it,
man? Speak up!"

"Why . . . my partner told me, and I have to agree.
This is the Princess of Dawson!"

"You are, aren't you?" cried the sourdough who'd
recognized her first. "It's really you, from the Palace
Grand Theater! Recited your father's poems . . . I musta
seen you a dozen times if I saw you once!"

The crowd was electrified.

"It's you, isn't it?" the grizzled prospector insisted.
"You used to be the Princess of Dawson. I'm sure it's
you."

The crowd hushed, all eyes on Jamie.

"That's me," she agreed.

A cheer went up from every throat. The word was
passed to those who hadn't been close enough to hear,
and the roar went down the street and back again.

"Wait a minute!" cried Donner. "What about the
rules? Produce the rules!"

"I have them right here," said the A.C.C. man,
pulling them out from among his papers.

Donner snatched the page away from him. "Right

here. Two-man teams. Two-*man* teams!"

For a moment the official hesitated. To his eternal credit, he thought it over for only a few seconds. Then he broke into a belly laugh that could be heard all the way to Dawson City.

"That's just an expression!" he roared.

"No, it's not!" thundered the boxer, who brandished his fist. "She can't be a girl. The race is only for men."

"All I can say is, fellows . . . if you were beaten by a girl, which you certainly were, then *more power to her*!"

The crowd went berserk. "The Princess of Dawson! The Princess of Dawson won the race!"

Amid the confusion, a fireplug of a man in an immaculate business suit approached Donner from the side. With a deft movement, he spun him off-balance, tripped him, put one knee on his back, and handcuffed him. "What is the meaning of this?" Donner cried from the side of his mouth.

Several men with badges appeared from the crowd and restrained Brackett.

"What is this all about?" yelled Donner from the ground.

The man who'd handcuffed him raised his voice for the crowd to hear. "It's about false identity, and worse."

"Explain, please," demanded the official from the Alaska Commercial Company.

"My name is John Tobin. I'm a detective with the Bartholomew and James Agency of Omaha, Nebraska. I arrived minutes ago from Dawson City aboard the *Eldorado*. I've been tracking this fellow who claims to be Cornelius Donner of Dawson City. He is actually George Swink of Jefferson City, Missouri, and he is wanted for murder and arson in two countries, the United States and Canada."

The detective stood Donner up and looked him in the eye. "For a year and a half, mister, I've been looking forward to this moment. You've put me through quite a bit of trouble, you have."

Donner—Swink, that is to say—spit in his face.

The crowd yelled its outrage. The detective wiped his face with a handkerchief and said calmly to Donner, "You'll need a good lawyer, mister. A mighty good lawyer."

As would have been the case in Dawson City, Nome turned out to be full of lawyers. Four were within earshot, and rushed forward to offer their services.

"I have nothing to pay with," Swink muttered. "All my assets are back in Dawson City."

"Impounded by the Canadian government, no doubt," put in the A.C.C. man.

"You'll be tried in Dawson City first," said the detective. "Then I'll take you back to Nebraska."

"I need a lawyer!" Donner cried. "A good one! Who'll represent me? I need an American!"

The four lawyers were about to turn heel. One of them said, "Nobody's working charity for the likes of you."

Now it was my time to step forward. "I think I can help you, George Swink. You need funds, and I need to get the Hawthorn Brothers Sawmill back. Remember?"

"Twenty thousand dollars!" he said with a look almost of triumph.

I shook my head. "That was your number, not mine."

"What's your number?"

"We'll have one of these lawyers draw up the papers—legal as can be, with witnesses and all. I'll give you three thousand dollars for the mill, which is the amount you loaned to my brother Ethan. We'll be fair and square."

"Three thousand dollars," he raged. "Who'll pay me more? It's worth far more! I have a saloon in Dawson as well!"

"The New Bodega," I said. I lowered my voice and said to Swink, "Should I tell everybody in Nome, loud and clear, that your partner died in the fire? Should I tell them that the arson you're accused of is the Great Fire?"

"Don't," the detective told me. "They'll lynch him dead."

The crowd had fallen to a hush, wondering what was being said. At last a wag shouted, "Give him three dollars, Hawthorn, not three thousand!"

Swink had as much room to negotiate as a mouse in a trap. A short while later, at the jail, he deeded over his entire interest in the mill for the sum of three thousand dollars, and not a dime more, to Abraham, Ethan, and Jason Hawthorn.

TWENTY–FOUR

During our stay in Nome, Jamie and I took rooms at the Golden Gate Hotel, Nome's finest. Once we'd bathed, slept out our exhaustion, and filled our stomachs, we strolled down the street shopping for clothes.

Same as Dawson, Nome had its personalities. Right away we heard that Wyatt Earp was in town, the famous marshall from the Wild West days in Dodge City, Kansas, and Tombstone, Arizona. In addition to owning a saloon, Earp was, of all things, a boxing promoter. Earp had already learned that the former heavyweight champion of the British Empire was in Nome and had signed him for a fight.

Jamie and I walked Nome's sprawling tent city and gazed like tourists at the sluice and rocker works and all the pits along the beach. Wherever the beach hadn't been dug, it was the staging ground for industry. Lumber was stacked high. So were mounds of coal, barrels of kerosene—everything that an instant city on the windswept, treeless tundra required. From the huge oceangoing steamers anchored offshore, freight lighters were arriving by the hour. Some were stacked with supplies, others crowded with hundreds of stampeders. Before the lighters even touched the beach, some people leapt into the shallows and took off sprinting, claim stakes in hand.

They were going to have to sprint a long, long way. We'd learned that the beach was already staked ten miles north and ten miles south, and so were the banks of the river as well as all the local creeks. And some of Nome's placers were proving out extremely rich. Indications were that Nome's first year would surpass even the Klondike's.

Everywhere we went, we were asked if we were going to stake a claim.

Jamie, in a bright new dress and scrubbed so clean she shined, would answer, "We're heading back to Dawson soon as possible. We're anxious to see Jason's brothers."

And so we were, but we had to wait out a storm that lashed Cape Nome for three days. It washed away the diggings all along the beach and destroyed a fortune in goods that couldn't be pulled from the waves in time. The shallow-drawing Yukon sternwheelers, able to moor in the mouth of the river, were spared.

As soon as the weather cleared, we boarded the *Eldorado*, which would take us across the sound and all the way up the Yukon to Dawson City.

After a pleasant few hours at Unalakleet, where we were able to present Father Karloff with a check on the Bank of Cape Nome for the amount of $6,700, the *Eldorado* steamed south to the old Russian port of St.

Michael. The following day we entered the northern-most channel of the Yukon. I was able to see those five hundred miles of the lower river I'd missed due to our portage. Jamie and I were both at the rail when Kaltag's few cabins appeared on the left bank. There was the greenish Kaltag River, where we'd paddled in among the salmon.

Though we never laid eyes on him, George Swink was on the *Eldorado*, too. John Tobin had him cuffed in a private room and never let him out among the passengers. I had no doubt he would be brought to justice.

Our return to Dawson City was a thoroughly joyous one. Jamie and I had quite a story to tell, and my brothers provided a most appreciative audience. As I described the last moments of the race, and the role Burnt Paw had played, that mongrel I'd named Nuisance proved a rapt listener. His ears were perked high, and his blue eye was staring at me as if to make sure I got it right.

When I came to the part about Burnt Paw tripping Jamie, his ears went down to half-mast. As I told of the pivotal moment when he tripped Donner, Ethan slapped himself on the leg so hard I was afraid he'd broken it all over again.

Abe, in his wry way, said to Ethan, "I seem to remember you calling him Underdog, or some such, before he was Burnt Paw."

"Yes, sir—watch your step—he's back in town!"

The first order of business, to my mind, was for the three of us to visit the mill and to have our name restored in large letters at the entrance. Before the day was out, we'd accomplished it.

While we were nailing the sign up at the mill, Jamie was paying a visit to Arizona Charlie Meadows. He did indeed want to buy her play, *The Adventures of Big Olaf McDoughnut.* She told him that she had a new character and a new scene to add, and he paid her five hundred dollars on the spot, with all terms as they'd agreed before.

The play made its debut three weeks later at the Palace Grand, with Klondikers by the hundreds roaring their approval. Jamie and the Hawthorn brothers were watching from seats in the third row. From his private box, Big Alex McDonald clapped and cheered and whistled every time his fictional counterpart entered a scene.

As I knew they would, Jamie's prospector jokes had the house roaring with laughter. But that wasn't the best part. The most popular scene in the play was all the more effective because so many in the audience knew it to be true. When Big Olaf McDoughnut invited the boy who'd lost his leg at the knee, Charlie Maguire, to reach into that glass bowl of nuggets and help himself, the young actor hesitated, then took very few nuggets, exactly as I remembered my friend Charlie doing in real life.

"No, no!" Big Olaf insisted. "I mean fill both trouser pockets full as you can get 'em, then your shirt pockets, too. Gold means nothing to me, lad. Nothing!"

At that, everyone in the theater rose, turned around, and applauded Big Alex McDonald, who saluted them modestly. I only wished Charlie could have been there to see it.

When the curtain came down on the play, the house erupted with deafening cheers for Jamie's celebration of the Klondike. When the curtain came up on the actors, and they were showered with flowers and nuggets, Arizona Charlie took the stage in buckskins, as always. The silver-haired frontiersman acknowledged the renewed applause, then motioned to Jamie several times—urgently—for her to come up and join him on the stage.

I could see what Arizona Charlie aimed to do—reduce the entire house to tears. He wanted Jamie beside him as he told of the passing of the poet of the Klondike, and how the author of the play they had just enjoyed was none other than the poet's daughter, the same girl many of them had known as the Princess of Dawson.

The man in buckskins beckoned to Jamie once more, but he had met his match. Firmly, she shook her head. The consummate showman, Arizona Charlie recovered before the audience even knew what had transpired. In a dramatic voice, he announced, "A hand for the playwright, Jamie Dunavant!" and pointed her way.

Jamie stood to acknowledge the cheers, gave the audience a wave and a golden smile, then sat down. "Whew!" she said, taking my hand. "I'd rather paddle the Norton Sound!"

Jamie's play kept the Palace Grand alive. By the end of the summer, some of the theaters and dance halls were closing. In one midsummer week alone, eight thousand people had left Dawson.

Some of the mills closed down, but not ours. We even kept it running through the winter.

Jamie lived in Melinda Mulrooney's Fairview Hotel, where she and her father had lived.

We saw each other every day. We were engaged to be married.

Jamie and I married several days after the ice broke on the Yukon. The day was June 1, 1900. I'd recently turned eighteen and Jamie seventeen. It was time. We were ready for the adventure.

A couple weeks later we embarked with Burnt Paw once again down the Yukon, this time in a handsome, river-worthy, twenty-five-foot skiff. We had a year's outfit on board with all the provisions and tools for getting started in the bush.

It was with a heart full of pride and love that I waved good-bye to my brothers that day in Dawson City. In the future, we'd come back to see them, or they'd come to find us, but it wouldn't be often. I suppose this was the way it was meant to be, with the two of them sticking together and me heading off over the northern horizon.

Dawson had a future, but on a far lesser scale than it had imagined itself, and much more civilized.

With Dawson so well connected to the Outside, it wasn't the place for Jamie and me. Our hearts were in the wilderness.

At the village of Koyukuk, just a mile up from the Yukon, we traded our skiff for seven husky pups, dog harnesses, a basket sled, and enough baled salmon to feed a team through the winter.

After a week a little sternwheeler arrived, and we started up the river of our dreams. The Koyukuk ran so clear we could see every stone on the bottom. At every village we asked after Johan and Ingrid Swenson. Everyone remembered them. Everyone kept pointing upriver.

We entered a country with vast stands of birch and aspen and tall spruce. Along the banks we saw moose, caribou, wolves, grizzly and black bear. The skies were teeming with birds. Hundreds of miles upriver we crossed the Arctic Circle. Mountains on both sides rising three thousand feet kept us from seeing the sun for several hours around midnight, not that we cared. We could climb one of these mountains any time we pleased for a view of the midnight sun.

We found our friends. The Swedes were surprised to see us—and pleased. Johan and Ingrid had settled at the mouth of the John River, only a few miles up the Koyukuk from a man named Gordon Bettles, who'd opened a store at the upstream limit of steamboat navigation. A new village named Bettles was taking shape around the store.

We settled at the mouth of the Wild River, next stream up from Johan and Ingrid and their children. They helped us pole our outfit up there in a boat they'd made from whipsawed lumber, and they helped us build our log cabin.

When winter came, we were ready.

There was a little gold in the creeks, and I meant to try my hand at it, but it wasn't gold that we or our friends were after. It was the independent life. Even without gold, the fishing, hunting, berrying, and gardening would pull us through.

Jamie and I were of one mind. Every day, summer and winter, would bring labor, but it would be meaningful labor in the midst of incomparable beauty and never lacking for adventure. We meant to raise our children in this place.

The first one came in October of 1901.

We named him Homer.

Our twins we named Rebeccah and Elizabeth, after our mothers, who died young.

Abraham and Ethan made five. To our good fortune, each one of our children survived, all of them healthy as weeds.

All the while Jamie was writing plays for the stage in Dawson and for Alaska's new gold mecca, Fairbanks.

Burnt Paw had a lot of years left in him. Summers he was always with me, up and down the river; when winter came, Jamie would outfit him with a knitted coat, and he never failed to come along.

A day rarely passed without a small war breaking out among our sled dogs, but for whatever reason they never laid a tooth on Burnt Paw. Maybe it was because he rode in the sled instead of pulling it; maybe it was because he lived in the cabin with us instead of out in the snow with them.

As time went by, Burnt Paw wasn't the leaper he once had been, nor the traveler. To his last days he favored that front right paw, and even little Ethan knew why. Burnt Paw's history was the stuff of legend. The children's pet was a sort of mythic hero, thanks to the bedtime stories their mother had fabricated over the years from his exploits in the mists of the previous century. When Jamie and I appeared in this saga it was infrequently, and as minor characters.

In his last few years, when Burnt Paw preferred to lie close to the stove and dream, the children thought we were lucky to still have the old fellow underfoot.

And so did I.

AUTHOR'S NOTE

In "The Spell of the Yukon," Robert W. Service wrote, "There's a land—oh, it beckons and beckons/And I want to go back—and I will."

That's exactly how I felt when I finished writing *Jason's Gold*, the story of Jason Hawthorn's eleven-month journey from New York City to Dawson City in 1897–98. My heart was still in the Northland; I had to go back and find out what came next for Jason. The result is *Down the Yukon*.

At the end of the first book Jamie had promised she'd come back, and there was so much left to explore—not only Jason and Jamie's relationship but the Yukon River itself. Together, the two of them might float clear across Alaska. The historical context, I realized, would be the 1899 rush to Cape Nome, where gold had been discovered in the beaches of the Bering Sea.

News of the discovery at Nome had an electrifying

effect on Dawson City. As many as eight thousand disappointed Klondikers left Dawson in a single week in
the summer of '99. Many of those were going to give it
one last try in Nome, and the Yukon was their highway
for most of the route.

In addition to those bound for salt water, there were
numbers of Klondikers who traveled down the Yukon
and then up virtually every one of its tributaries, searching Alaska for a new bonanza or simply a place to live
in the wilderness. Some of these settled far up the
Koyukuk River, even north of the Arctic Circle.

I've had a longtime fascination with the Koyukuk
that came from reading books by two acclaimed conser-
vationists, Margaret Murie and Robert Marshall, who
knew the river intimately. Mardy Murie's book is *Two in
the Far North* (Alaska Northwest Books, 1997 reprint)
and Bob Marshall's is *Arctic Village* (University of
Alaska Press, 1993 reprint).

In the early 1930s, Bob Marshall spent over a year in
the settlement of Wiseman, upstream of Bettles. Some of
its old-timers were Klondikers who'd left Dawson City in
the summer of 1899. Marshall described Wiseman's
small community of many races as "the happiest civilization of which I have knowledge." Wishing great hap-
piness for Jason and Jamie, I had them settle on the
upper Koyukuk.

As in *Jason's Gold,* I strove to describe the geography
and landscapes of *Down the Yukon* as accurately as possible. In regard to the plausibility of Yukon River sternwheelers managing the crossing of Norton Sound, I was
amazed to read accounts of them moored in the mouth
of the river at Nome, and then to find 1899 photographs
depicting exactly that.

The idea of the attempt to float a hotel down the

Yukon came from Arizona Charlie Meadows's announcement in real life that he would float his Palace Grand Theater in one piece from Dawson City to Nome. He abandoned the idea. Destroyed in the April fire of '99, the Palace Grand reopened in July, and remains standing today under another name.

Henry Brackett, the Sydney Mauler, is a fictional counterpart of an actual Australian boxer named Frank Slavin ("Sydney Cornstalk") who fought a number of matches in Dawson City and was a former heavyweight champion of the British Empire. The subplot involving George Swink, a.k.a. Cornelius Donner, was inspired by a true-life twenty-five-thousand-mile detective saga involving arson and murder that began in Iowa and ended in Dawson City. The actual criminal's name was Frank Novak, and the detective was C. C. Perrin.

Dawson's Thanksgiving fire of '98 and the April 26 fire of '99 took place largely as described in the novel, though arson was not suspected in either event.

The names in *Down the Yukon* of Dawson's dance halls, theaters, gambling houses, saloons, banks, and hotels are the actual ones. I have portrayed or referred to many of Dawson's colorful historical characters in their actual context. These include Arizona Charlie Meadows, Irish Nellie Cashman, Little Margie Newman, Belinda Mulrooney, Calamity Jane, Joe Boyle, Big Alex McDonald, Swiftwater Bill Gates, Joseph Ladue, Buckskin Frank Leslie, George Washington Carmack, Dick Lowe, Jack Dalton, Captain Starnes, Waterfront Brown, Silent Sam Bonnifield, Louis Golden, One-Eyed Riley, Hamgrease Jimmy, the Evaporated Kid, and others. Incidentally, Wyatt Earp of Dodge City fame indeed surfaced in Nome as a saloon owner and boxing promoter.

Jason and Jamie, as well as Jason's brothers, Abe and Ethan, are entirely fictional. Burnt Paw's name is drawn from that of a village on the Porcupine River.

The North American Trading and Transportation Company and the Alaska Commercial Company are the names of the actual companies that supplied Dawson City and Nome. The idea of the former's breakup lottery was inspired by the annual lottery on the exact time of breakup on the Tanana River, which I recalled from my childhood in Alaska. The Great Race from Dawson City to Nome, sponsored by the Alaska Commercial Company, is fictional. The ancient portage trail between Kaltag on the Yukon River and Unalakleet on the Bering Sea is real. In modern times it is a section of the Iditarod dogsled race, which ends in Nome.

Once again I am indebted to Pierre Berton's superb history *Klondike: The Last Great Gold Rush, 1896–1899* (Penguin, 1990 reprint). I would also point interested readers to William Haskell's period narrative, *Two Years in the Klondike and Alaskan Gold-Fields 1896–1898* (University of Alaska Press, 1997 reprint); *Women of the Klondike,* by Frances Backhouse (Whitecap Books, 1995); *The Miners,* by Robert Wallace, with photographs (Time/Life Books, 1976); *The Alaskans,* by Keith Wheeler, with photographs (Time/Life Books, 1977); *Reading the River: A Voyage Down the Yukon,* by John Hildebrand (Houghton Mifflin, 1988); and *The Klondike Gold Rush—Photographs from 1896–99* (Wolf Creek Books, 1997).

As was the case with *Jason's Gold,* I was writing *Down the Yukon* exactly one hundred years after its events took place. My wife, Jean, and I hope to revisit Dawson City one of these years, and I have my heart set on seeing the Koyukuk River north of the Arctic Circle.

I'd like to visit the setting that moved Bob Marshall to write these words: "It is impossible ever to evaluate just how much beauty adds to what is worthwhile in existence."

Durango, Colorado
August 1999